FLIPPING TAILS FOR SEASICK MERMAIDS

OBSCURE ACADEMY #4

LAURA GREENWOOD

BLURB

Fiona has always feared the ocean, and it's only become worse since she drowned and became a mermaid.

Wade has spent the past few years as a swimming instructor to help pay for his studies, but the last thing he expects is to find a gorgeous mermaid asking him to teach her too.

Can Fiona overcome her fear of water long enough to realise there might be something more between them?

-

Flipping Tails For Seasick Mermaids is a light-hearted mermaid & merman academy m/f romance set at Obscure Academy. It is Fiona and Wade's complete story.

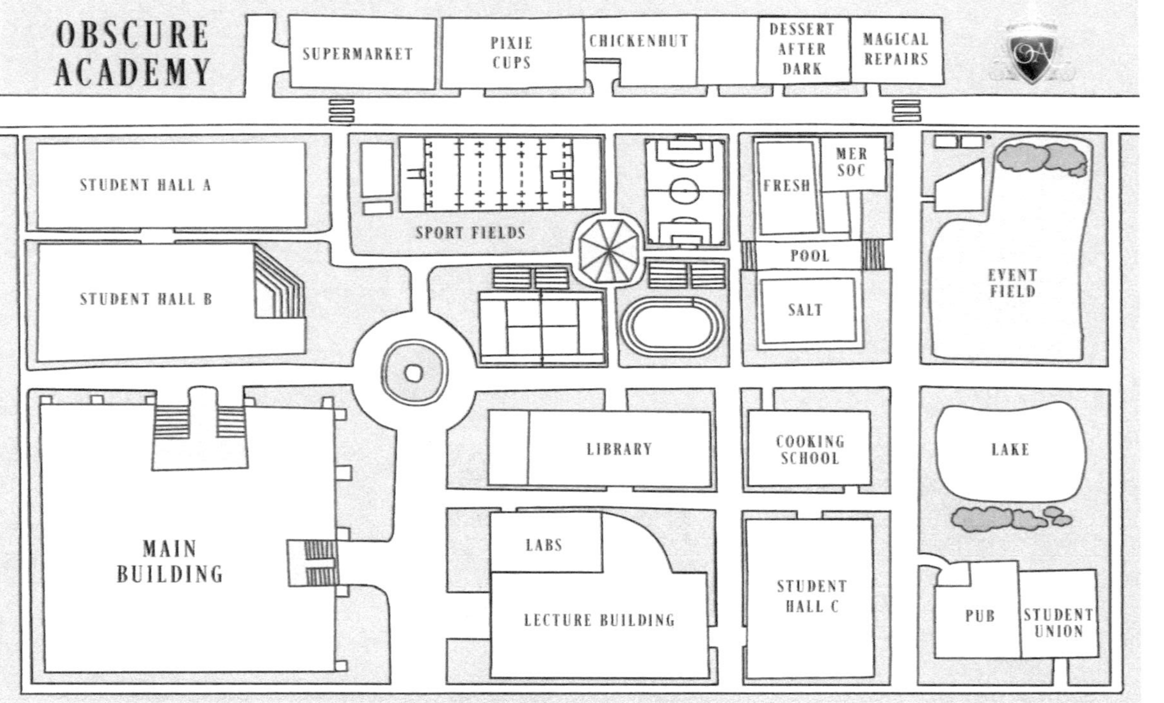

OBSCURE ACADEMY
SUPERMARKET
PIXIE CUPS
CHICKENHUT
DESSERT AFTER DARK
MAGICAL REPAIRS
STUDENT HALL A
STUDENT HALL B
SPORT FIELDS
FRESH
MER SOC
POOL
SALT
EVENT FIELD
LIBRARY
COOKING SCHOOL
LAKE
MAIN BUILDING
LABS
LECTURE BUILDING
STUDENT HALL C
PUB
STUDENT UNION
HTTPS://WWW.AUTHORLAURAGREENWOOD.CO.UK

ONE

FIONA

THE FAMILIAR SCENT of salt fills the air, coming off the pool in waves. While I've spent a good part of my life trying to avoid anything that makes me think of the sea, I've grown used to the smell over the past couple of months, and have even come to find it a little comforting.

I close my eyes and inhale, taking it in and trying to pluck up the courage to join the mer in the water.

"You okay, Fi?" Georgie asks as she hoists herself out of the water and sits beside me. Her long tail flicks back and forth, the bluish hint to her scales glittering in the light from overhead.

"Just thinking."

"You know you're not supposed to do too much of that, it's dangerous."

I chuckle. "We're students, we're supposed to think."

"Sure, during class. But not during MerSoc."

I smile and swish my legs back and forth, enjoying the way the water feels against them even if there is a longing to let my scales take over and my tail spring forth. It's a cruel twist of fate that I long for the touch of water so much.

"Do you not want to get your tail out?" Georgie asks, gesturing to my legs.

I shake my head. "Maybe next week."

She lets out a good-natured laugh. "One day, next week is actually going to come," she teases.

"Maybe."

"Even Melody showed us hers," she says. "Where is she, anyway?"

"No idea, maybe she's hanging out with Josh tonight? She did say something about meeting his parents," I respond. Normally I can count on Melody to sit on the side with me during MerSoc meetings, though her reasons are different to mine.

"Ah, yeah, that could be it," Georgie responds.

"And don't worry about your tail. These things take some mer time. No one here wants you to be uncomfortable."

"I know," I assure her. I've been coming to MerSoc for months and it's fun to be here, even when everyone is talking about the upcoming trip to Merton that I know I can't go on. At least with some of the subspecies of mer around it's not weird for me to not have my tail out, though thanks to my hair, there's no hiding what kind of mer I am. Sometimes I envy the sirens and merrows for having more human shades.

Georgie lets out a loud sigh, drawing my attention back to her.

"Everything all right?" I ask.

She nods. "It just looks like Ben and Felix are about to get into a fight again." She nods towards the two mermen.

"I wonder what it's about this time?" They always seem to be getting into it with one another.

"With those two, who knows? I've always had this theory that they fight so much because there's something else physical they'd rather be doing."

I raise an eyebrow. "Then why don't they?"

"Honestly, I'm not sure. It would solve a lot of my problems. I have to go keep the peace. You'll be all right on your own?"

"I always am," I assure her. Though it's much more fun when she or Melody are here for me to hang out with, I don't mind being alone. I'm used to it after years being the only mer in school.

"Hmm." Something catches her eye and a knowing smile spreads over her face. "It looks like you won't be alone for long anyway. Have fun and don't do anything I wouldn't." There's a mischievous twinkle in her eye, but before I can ask what it's about, she dives back into the water, splashing me with refreshing droplets.

I shake my head in bemusement. Georgie is always so confident and sure of herself, and I feel like I'm neither. Despite that, we seem to have become firm friends since meeting a few months back, of which I'm glad. No one else is as patient with my constant questions about mer society.

"Hey," a voice I don't recognise says.

I look up.

"Do you want this one? I noticed you don't have a drink." A guy with piercing blue eyes stands next to me with a can of pre-mixed cocktail in his hand, offering it to me.

"Thank you." I reach out and take it from him without thinking too much about it. The whole point of being part of MerSoc is that I talk to other mer and become their friends.

"Can I sit?" He gestures to the side of the pool beside me.

"Of course." I open my can and take a sip. "Thanks for the drink."

"You're welcome." He sits next to me and flashes me a reassuring smile. "I'm Wade."

"Fiona."

"Ah, yes, Georgie said we had a few new members this year." He swings his legs back and forth in the water, but doesn't get his tail out.

"You were already a member of MerSoc?"

He nods. "I joined last year."

"Oh, I assumed you were new, I haven't seen you around before."

"I normally teach a class around now," Wade admits.

"A class? You're a teacher?" I didn't think they'd be allowed to join a student society.

Wade chuckles, the sound filling the air pleasantly. "I wouldn't go that far. I'm a swimming instructor," he says. "I started working at the local pool when I was in my final year of school, and I've just continued now I'm here."

"Oh." Somehow, the idea of a merman being a swimming instructor makes a lot of sense, but isn't something I've ever thought about before. "Do you enjoy it?"

He takes a sip of his drink before responding. "Sort of. It isn't my dream job, but I love seeing the kids' faces when they realise they're able to do a length of the pool for the first time."

"That's sweet."

"I've never actually told anyone that before," he says. "I always thought it made me sound creepy."

I let out a light laugh. "Saying you think it makes you sound creepy makes it sound creepy."

"Ah, I should work on that." A boyish grin lights up his face, helping to put me more at ease than I've been with a lot of people.

"Do you only teach kids?" I ask, a plan forming in my mind that is only partly based on the fact he has kind eyes and feels nice to talk to, even if it's barely been five minutes.

"Yes. Why? Do you know someone?"

Embarrassment threatens to overtake me, but I push it to the side. I'm never going to be able to go on MerSoc trips if I don't learn how to swim.

"If you don't teach adults, it's okay," I respond quickly, dismissing my idea as a foolish one.

"I don't think they'd be able to come to the classes, but I could do a private session for them," he says. "I can give you my number if you want to pass it on to them?"

"It's me," I blurt before checking around to make sure no one else is listening. "I can't swim."

He raises an eyebrow, but manages to just about hide the shock that flashes through his eyes. "I see."

"I need to learn." Though realistically, it's eight years too late for that. I push the thought to the side. I can rectify the mistake and not drown the next time I'm in the water.

"We can do a lesson," he says firmly. "How about Friday at four? The pool here is free then, so we can use it."

"You'll just do it like that?"

"Yes."

"But, why? You don't know me." A small part of me expected him to reject the notion simply based on the fact I can't swim, but apparently, he's not going to.

"Maybe I want to change that." The way he smiles at me makes my heart skip a beat.

This better not develop into an ill-advised crush. That's the last thing I need.

"All right. Friday at four," I respond. "Thank you."

"You're welcome."

"Hey, Wade," Brad shouts from across the pool. "We're about to play water polo, do you want in?"

"Sure," he calls back.

"Want to join, Fiona?" Brad asks.

I shake my head. "I'll sit this one out, I don't know the rules yet."

Wade shoots me a look, before putting the pieces together. "Cheer me on from the side?"

"Of course." I hold up my drink in a fake toast.

He gets to his feet and heads to the other end of the pool where the others are already waiting to play. I look down at my drink, unsure whether what I've just agreed to is a good idea or not.

On the one hand, I need to learn how to swim, especially if I don't want to continue standing out at MerSoc events. On the other, I don't know Wade, and I'm trusting him with my biggest secret just because he brought me a drink.

A loud splash pulls my attention back to the pool. Half a dozen mer are now sitting on the sides of the pool, giving the space over to the two teams of seven who are setting up to begin their game. I really should learn the rules, they play almost every week.

Despite sometimes feeling like I don't belong amongst the others, there's something nice about being a part of MerSoc. It makes me feel as if I'm a bit less weird.

Hopefully, learning to swim will make me even more at home in the pool.

TWO

FIONA

THE KITCHEN IS full to bursting with my flatmates. Well, seven of them. We invited Craig to our regular flat night out, but as normal, no one has seen or heard anything from him. Sometimes, I find it hard to believe a ninth person lives here.

"We should do some shots," Michaela announces loudly.

Krissi groans. "I'm not sure I can stand up to go get them, Mickie."

"That's not a problem." Mickie pulls out her wand and waves it in the direction of a bottle of tequila, making it float through the air haphazardly until it comes to rest in the middle.

"Handy. Can you get some lime too?" Bernie asks. "Tequila is *always* better with lime."

"Tequila is best when no one has to drink it," I correct the vampire.

She chuckles. "You're such a spoilsport. For that, you're going to have to do the first one." She grabs the bottle and sloshes some of the amber liquid into it before pushing it in my direction.

"What, no lime?" I ask.

She lets out a loud cackle. "Nope. You mocked the tequila shots, you have to take one without any of the extras. Drink up."

I eye the shot glass warily, wondering if this is going to be a mistake.

"Fionaaaaaaaaaaaa, you have to do it," Mickie says.

"Fine. But if it makes me sick, you're the one who has to clean it up."

"All it'll take is a flick of my wand." She waves it around as if to illustrate her point.

Krissi grabs it out of her hand. "You're going to poke someone's eye out with that."

"Hey, no fair. You can't just take my wand." Mickie crosses her arms across her chest and pulls a face at the leopard shifter holding it just out of reach.

"You can have it back when I'm sure you're not going to magic everywhere."

I let out an amused snort, hoping their antics are enough to distract them all from the shot in front of me.

"Wait, wasn't Fiona supposed to be doing the first tequila?" Cyprus asks from further down the table.

I suppress a groan. Now the guys are involved, there isn't going to be any way of me getting away with not doing it.

I pick up the shot glass and toast them before throwing it back. It burns and makes me want to gag, but I manage to get it down.

My flatmates cheer louder than they should.

"Eurgh, that's awful," I mutter.

"But now you've paid your penalty, you get to choose who does it next," Bernie responds with a grin.

"Well you'll clearly enjoy it too much," I muse. And if Krissi drinks too much, she won't make it out of the flat, which means Jeremy will probably stay behind to take care of her too. I'm glad they got over their refusal to get together, but they can be sickeningly sweet together. "Shots were Mickie's idea, she should be the one who does the next one," I announce with certainty.

"Or we could all do them together?" Essie responds, already lining up eight shot glasses.

"Wait, that's not fair, I already did mine," I protest.

She throws me an amused look.

I sit back in my seat and wait for the inevitable, thinking about how strange it is for me to be so comfortable around these people. I've only known them for a few months, and we all have lives outside the flat, but there's a camaraderie I've never felt with anyone else before.

Around them, I can be completely me. I don't have to think about the fact I don't fit in with the mer, or that I'm not quite human either. Everyone around this table is supernatural, but they're all different at the same time.

And not one of them is thinking about the terrible impression I made on a hot merman by blurting out that I can't swim in front of him.

"Earth to Fionaaaaaaa," Bernie sing-songs. "What's up with you?"

"Oh, I know that face," Essie says brightly. "It's the same one you got on yours when you met Shane."

"It is!" Mickie agrees. "And the one Krissi and Jeremy had for months. That was painful to watch."

"Hey!" Krissi protests.

"I'm just saying it like it is," the witch responds with a shrug.

For a moment, it looks like Krissi is about to argue, but she decides against it and leans back against Jeremy. The auburn-haired tiger shifter puts an arm around her.

"They have a point," he says.

Krissi tries to glare at him, but doesn't manage to look particularly scary.

"Are you dating someone you haven't told us about?" Bernie asks me, breaking through my hope that the conversation will have moved on from me.

"I'm not dating anyone," I assure them.

"If you are, I can give you some tips on sneaking out unnoticed," Essie suggests.

Cyprus lets out a loud laugh. "No one would take that advice, Ess, you're as subtle as a vampire in a blood bath when it comes to sneaking out your conquests."

"That's very unfair to Bernie," Essie counters. "You shouldn't use that expression."

Cyprus turns his attention to the vampire.

She shrugs. "It's a good analogy," she agrees

before turning her attention to Essie more fully. "How is Byron, anyway?"

The fae's cheeks flame red. "Fine, as far as I know," she mutters under her breath.

I share an amused look with Michaela. Essie *claims* she's over ending things with him, and that it didn't mean anything anyway, but I'm not convinced she's being entirely truthful with herself.

"So, who are they?" Mickie asks me. "The person that's got you daydreaming in the middle of pre-drinks."

Wade's friendly face crosses my mind, but I push the thought to the side. We've only had one conversation, and yet I'm looking forward to our swimming lesson tomorrow more than I've ever looked forward to going near water. "No one."

She raises an eyebrow. "I'm not sure I believe you."

"How about I do an extra shot and you all stop asking me questions?" I suggest, pulling one of the glasses towards me before any of them can argue.

"Now I'm more convinced than ever," Bernie says. "But you can keep your secrets in exchange for tequila."

"I'm going to regret this in the morning," I mumble as I sprinkle salt onto my hand. If I'm going to do another shot, then I'm going to do it properly this time.

I take a deep breath and lick the salt and knock the shot back in a few swift moments. I hold out my hand and gesture for one of the limes. I don't even pay attention to which one of them gives me and just shove it in my mouth, using the sharp tang of the juice to get rid of the tequila taste.

"Ahhh, who invented tequila?" I lament.

The others pass the salt around and take their shots, and I have to admit that an unforeseen advantage of going first is that I get to see the assortment of faces they pull as they do.

I pick up my rum and coke and take a sip, much preferring it to the shots. A pleasant buzz surrounds me, though I think the company has a lot to do with that as well as the alcohol.

"Should we book the taxis to the club?" Cyprus asks. "For eleven?"

"Eleven is good," Bernie agrees. "The club has half-price tickets until half-past."

Which gives us enough time to get in before the place gets too busy. And then we'll spend hours dancing away and having a blast.

It's going to be a good night, and well worth the potential headache in the morning.

THREE

FIONA

I SWAY BACK AND FORTH, trying to ignore the woozy feeling in my head as I make my way down the corridor and towards my room. My feet hurt from dancing all night, and I've definitely drunk too much.

"Fiona, you have to be careful," Mickie admonishes as she follows me.

I shake my head. "I'm fineeee."

"You're not fine," she counters. "You're very drunk." She sounds a little worried, though I'm not exactly sure why when she's had as much to drink as I have.

"That's because you made me do shots." And now the fun part of drinking is over and I have to find my way to bed. I push my bedroom door open, glad I thought to leave it unlocked when we left earlier. Though now I think about it, that may not have been purposeful.

She sighs and follows me inside. "How can we sober you up?" she asks. "Does shifting work for you like it does for Krissi?"

"I don't think it's called shifting," I mumble. "But no one has ever told me what I'm supposed to call it. Is it fishing? I'm going to fish-out." I turn and head towards my bathroom, catching myself on the doorframe as I stumble past.

Mickie hurries after, but I don't pay her any attention as I knock the shower on and let the water tumble down to the floor.

"What..."

"I'm fishing-out," I respond before she can finish.

I lower myself into the shower and lean my back against the wall, not bothering to remove my dress. I close my eyes and position my head up so the water touches it. I'm not sure exactly what triggers it, or if it just happens because I want it to, but my tail bursts forth, replacing my legs. I swish it about in the water, enjoying the way it feels against my scales.

I let out a loud sigh. "Perfect."

"Is this going to help you get sober?" Mickie sits on the toilet seat so our conversation doesn't have to end.

I shrug. "Not sure. I haven't tried it before, but then I sometimes try and avoid fishing-out. But you said it worked with Krissi."

She nods. "At least, I think so. She shifted into her leopard form while drunk a couple of months ago and it stopped her getting a hangover. Maybe it'll work for you too."

"And then maybe I'll drink more," I mutter.

A frown pulls at her features. "Why do you want to drink more?"

"To forget."

"That's not a good reason."

"In fairness, I never said it was a good reason, just that it was *a* reason." And not one I've ever actually used, but that doesn't seem to matter to me right now.

"What do you need to forget?" she asks instead of continuing down that path. Mickie is so smart, even if she's terrible at making tea.

"That I can't swim," I admit. It feels good to say it out loud for the second time in as many days, especially when I've been keeping it quiet for so long.

She blinks a few times, not seeming to take me seriously, and I can understand why. I'm a mermaid who can't swim, it isn't exactly a common predicament.

"How can you not swim?" she asks. "Weren't you born with the ability?"

"Were you?"

"Well, no. But I'm a witch."

"And I was human. Though I suppose some babies can swim straight away if it's a water birth. But I was just born the standard way, I think."

Mickie stares at me. "You were born human?"

"Mmhmm." I splash my tail against the floor, sending a few shoots of water up into the air. This is surprisingly fun. I should do this more often.

"But you have a tail."

"Well noticed," I mutter. "Mer are like vampires, they can be born or they can be made. Kind of. It's not really like vampires either. It isn't another mer who decides, it's the sea. I think. It's confusing and I haven't asked too many questions about it."

"What happened?"

I bite my bottom lip. Do I really want to go into this? I know I started it, but that doesn't make it an easy thing to talk about. Then again, maybe it's a good thing if I do. It'll help me get past some of the feelings I have about it.

"I don't know where to begin," I admit. "I've never told anyone about it."

"It's okay if you don't want to," she says softly.

I shake my head. "I think I'm ready to."

"Even though you've been drinking? I'm happy to listen, but I don't want you to regret it in the morning," she says, revealing more of her thoughtfulness even if she's just as drunk as I am.

"That makes it easier."

"Okay." She waits for me to continue, not pushing me, and just waiting.

I take a deep breath and listen to the soothing sound of the water against the tiles. "I drowned. I was ten and my brother and I were playing on a pier. One of the boards broke, and I fell through." A shiver runs down my spine as I recall the way it felt to crash into the cold water from that height.

I lift my hand to my throat, feeling the echo of a scream long passed.

I push it away. It's best if I don't dwell on the specifics, especially if I don't want to end up giving myself nightmares.

"I'm not really sure what happened after that. I remember crying and begging the sea to spare me. Everything went dark, and the next thing I knew, I was on the beach with a tail." I gesture to it. "I think it's a flying fish tail."

"What?"

"A quirk of mer-tails that I never knew until recently, they all match a real type of fish. It took a lot of staring at fish pictures for me to work it out." After I learned the truth from Georgie, I spent several days looking at all kinds of fish and trying to find examples of them as mer-tails to work it out. I may be wrong, but I don't think so.

"Huh, I had no idea," Mickie responds.

"Then again, how many mer-tails have you seen?"

"Good point, yours is the first unless you count the ones on TV."

"It was the same for me until I came here," I admit. "I've never known any other mer. It's been eye-opening."

"I'm glad you've found some answers," she says softly.

"Thanks. Me too. But it comes with some problems."

"Like not knowing how to swim?"

"Exactly. No one knows, but it's only a matter of time before they work out why I'm not going in the pool." Well, I suppose two people know. Which is enough as far as I'm concerned.

"Did you know before you..." she trails off, presumably not wanting to say the word.

"Drowned?" I finish for her. "No. I was angry at my parents for not making me learn before. Most kids seem to have lessons before then. How old were you?"

"I don't remember," Mickie admits. "Six or seven, I think."

"Exactly. I should have been able to swim by ten. But I couldn't, and maybe that's why this happened to me. Or it could have happened anyway. The sea is the sea. It clearly wanted me to be mer, and I'm grateful for that in a lot of ways. It's given me a chance at life that I might not have had otherwise."

"It's understandably conflicting."

I nod. "Anyway, so now I need to learn to swim."

"Have you never thought about learning before?"

"Several times," I admit, swirling my hand through the water next to me. "But every time I get to the point of going in the water, I can't make myself do it. I haven't had a bath in eight years."

"You're showering now." She gestures to the water.

"Yes. And I can sit by a pool. I can even put my feet in now, but I never used to be able to."

"Is there anything we can do to help?"

I don't need to ask to know who *we* is. She'll pull

the whole flat into solving the problem if I ask her to. Well, except for Craig, but that's because we've still never seen him.

"I found a teacher," I assure her.

"Another mer?"

I nod and a small blush rises to my cheeks.

Mickie chuckles. "An attractive mer?"

"Very," I mutter. "But I doubt he's going to find me attractive once he realises how bad the situation is."

"Then he's blind and an idiot," Mickie assures me. "And not worth your time. Other than swimming lessons."

I chuckle. "True. So long as I get what I want out of the situation, it's fine, right?"

"It is."

I stare down at the water, enjoying the way the droplets slip down my tail and to the ground. My dress is soaked, but I don't think it matters too much, it's the same water the washing machine uses anyway, it won't ruin it.

As I watch another bead of water trail down my scales, I realise my head isn't spinning nearly as much as it was.

"Hey, it looks like fishing-out sobered me up after all," I joke.

"So it seems," Mickie agrees. "Though perhaps it was also the serious conversation."

"Maybe." I don't think it really matters. Whatever has caused it, I'm not feeling the effects of drinking nearly as much as I was. "Thank you, Mickie."

She smiles reassuringly at me. "Any time, Fiona. I mean it. And I want to know how your swimming lessons get on, it'll make a difference where we go during the summer."

"You really think we're going to go on a trip together over the holidays?"

"Yep. I've had so much fun with you guys over the past couple of months that I'm going to make it happen," she assures me. "If you're up for being near the sea again, we could hire a house near the beach and have one long party."

I chuckle. "We still have another six months and some exams to get through first," I remind her.

"And this is how I plan on getting through the revision schedule I'm going to need."

I chuckle. "Fair point." The water starts to turn cold and a shiver runs through me. I reach up and shut off the shower, my tail almost instantly turning back to legs in the process. "I guess that's the facilities telling us it's time to sleep."

She lets out a light laugh. "I think you might be

right." She gets up and hands me my towel. "I'll see you tomorrow."

"Sleep well."

She waves and leaves the bathroom.

I strip off my dress and underwear, throwing them to the shower floor. They're too wet to put in my wash basket, which means I'll have to deal with them in the morning.

I wrap the towel around myself and head back out into my room. My bed looks more inviting than ever, and I flop down onto it, letting sleep take me.

FOUR

WADE

I'M NOT sure whether to be more excited or nervous about the upcoming swimming lesson, though I'm never going to admit it out loud. The last thing I want is to make Fiona uncomfortable. Especially as I know the reason I agreed to this wasn't exactly a professional one.

A part of me hopes that she's not going to show up then I don't have to deal with that.

The door to the pool swings open and she walks in wearing a button-down dress and looking like she's caught in the headlights. She's clearly just as nervous as I thought she would be about this, and everything about her screams the truth in her statement that she isn't able to swim.

A small part of me is excited that it'll mean more one-on-one time with her while I help her learn.

"Hey," she says with a nervous wave.

"Hi." I smile reassuringly at her. "Ready for your first lesson?"

She glances at the pool, a note of apprehension in her eyes.

"I'm ready," she says with a certainty I don't think she feels.

I nod, not completely believing her, but knowing this is going to be a tough journey. There are very few reasons for a mer not to know how to swim, and all of them are traumatic in one way or another.

"So, where do we start?" she asks, a determined expression crossing her face.

"We should get in the water," I respond.

"Right." She heads closer to it and then looks back at me.

I grab the bottom of my shirt and pull it over my head, dropping it to the side.

Her eyes widen and for the briefest moment, her gaze slips down to my chest and I enjoy the attention. Fiona gulps and wraps her arms around herself.

"Do we have to..." She gestures to her clothes.

"Don't you normally take your clothes off to swim?" I ask, before realising what a dumb question that is when she's already told me she doesn't know-how. "Sorry."

"It's okay. I'm just not used to this," she admits.

"We can go one step at a time," I promise her, realising I'm probably going a little bit too fast for what she's comfortable with.

She reaches up and pushes a strand of shimmery green hair behind her ear. "I'd like that."

"If you'd rather stay dressed, we can do that," I promise. I grab my shirt from the ground and pull it over my head again.

"What are you doing?" she asks, curiosity coming through her tone.

"Putting my shirt back on."

"Oh. Is the lesson over?" Her disappointment is written all over her face, though I don't know if it's because I've covered my chest or because she fears I'm ending the lesson.

I suppose both of those are good news to me. I want to have the beautiful mermaid's attention on me.

"No, I just thought it might make you more comfortable if I was wearing something too." I head towards the water, and sit down, only pulling my trunks off once the water has covered me. I wouldn't normally bother waiting until I'm in the water with another mer. My scales cover everything important, even when I'm in my human form, but she doesn't seem used to any of this and as the person she's trusted to teach her to swim, I need to make sure she's comfortable above all else.

I let the feel of the water bring forth my tail, the scales spreading down until they end in a fin at the end. I swish my tail back and forth, enjoying the way it feels.

"You can join me when you're ready," I tell her.

Slowly, she makes her way over and steps into the water. Tension rolls off her in waves, and I find myself wishing that I could make it easier for her. But without knowing what's causing the problems, or why she's never learned to swim, I can't do much.

She sits down and stretches her legs out. Within seconds, they're replaced by a graceful tail with multiple fins.

I raise an eyebrow. "A flying fish tail."

"You recognise it?" she asks, staring at her tail as if she's never seen it before.

I nod. "I do, but they aren't common around here. I've mostly seen them on mer when I'm on holiday."

"Oh." Her fins float in an ethereal way, and her

scales glitter in the warm afternoon sunshine. "What kind of tail is yours? Or is it rude to ask that?"

"You haven't spent much time around other merfolk, have you?"

She shakes her head. "I didn't knowingly meet another mer until I came here. I've learned a lot in a short space of time, but I still feel like I'm missing so much."

"You can ask me anything you want."

"Aren't I supposed to be learning how to swim?"

"Do you want to go deeper?"

Panic flits across her face, making me long to reach out and offer her some kind of physical comfort.

"It's okay. I thought we'd just sit here and help you get used to the water for a while," I assure her. "Then we can move a bit deeper and do the same there."

"Oh. That sounds good."

Relief flits through me. At least I actually seem to be helping her. And a small part of me is glad it seems like this is going to take a while. I want to get to know her, and spending one-on-one time together is going to help with that.

"I do have a question," Fiona says.

"I'm all ears." And curious about what she's going to ask.

"People seem to use merfolk and mer interchangeably, is there a difference?"

"There is," I respond. "All mer are merfolk, not all merfolk are mer."

"You're going to have to explain that one."

"Right, sorry." I need to remember that she's new to all of this. "You're mer. It's what people traditionally think of when you say mermaid or merman. We have multi-coloured tails and our hair often matches."

"Yeah, I noticed that. Not very helpful if you're trying to go under the radar."

"Mmm, true. Anyway, then you have other types of merfolk. Sirens, merrows, ceasgs, rusalkas, renyus, ningyos, and some others are all merfolk. They share characteristics with us, and each other, but they're not technically the same species as mer."

"Right. Like sirens need to sing in order to access their tails, but we don't."

I raise an eyebrow, surprised she knows that.

"One of my friends is a siren," Fiona explains.

"Huh, they're not normally that talkative," I respond. "But anyway, it's hard for people to tell the differences when they aren't merfolk themselves, and sometimes even if they are, so the terms ended up becoming interchangeable."

"That makes sense." She leans back. "But I bet they all know how to swim."

"I suspect there's a range of swimming abilities." Though she's right, I imagine there are very few merfolk who don't know how.

"Hmm."

"Have you had any swimming lessons before?" I ask.

"Never. Well, not never. Kind of never." She sighs and hides her face in her hands before sighing. "I'm sorry, I'm not making this very easy for you."

"It's fine," I assure her. "I've had students who were scared of the water before."

"I'm not...no, that's a lie. I am scared of the water. I bet they weren't eighteen though."

"Only because none of my students are," I point out, though I have to admit that an eighteen-year-old mermaid who can't swim isn't exactly common. "And it doesn't matter how old you are. It's brave to face a fear."

She gives me a hesitant smile. "I had a swimming lesson once, after, well after this." She waves her hands in the direction of her tail.

I can fill in the blanks.

"How did it go?"

"Very badly. I think it was a mistake to try and approach a human swimming instructor."

"Did you tell them you were mer?"

"It didn't get that far," she admits. "It was a very bad lesson. I didn't even make it into the water."

"And it put you off."

"Exactly."

"So I guess the real question is why do you want to learn now?"

She glances away, swishing her hand through the water. The way she does it is reminiscent of most merfolk I know, which makes me think she'll take to the water well in the end. It'll just take some time for her to get there.

"You don't have to tell me if you don't want," I say quickly. "I just thought it might help if we talk about these things."

She lets out a loud sigh. "I think it will, I'm just so used to *not* talking about it."

My heart aches for her. I'm not going to pry too much into what she went through after she became mer, but I suspect it's as bad as some of the other horror stories I've heard.

"Everyone at MerSoc was talking about the upcoming trip to Merton, and I realised I didn't have the option to say yes, even if I wanted to."

"Ah, I see."

"But I might have a bigger problem than the swimming."

"What might be a bigger problem?"

"I get seasick," she mumbles.

"Ah, that's common among freshwater mer," I respond kindly.

"But flying fish are from the sea."

"True. But you used to be human. I've never talked to any other turned mer about it, but I suspect it might be a common side effect. Have you ever tried taking human seasickness medication for it?"

Fiona frowns. "No, I worried that it would mess with something that shouldn't be messed with."

"A wise decision. But you'd be fine. If it worked when you were human, it'll still work now."

"That seems like a really low-tech solution."

"Sometimes, the things that work are the simple ones," I respond. "And you might not even need one for Merton. It isn't in the sea."

"It's not?"

He shakes his head. "It's in an estuary."

"Oh. I had no idea."

"I didn't think so."

"How am I ever going to fit in with the other mer when I don't even know the basics?" Her voice cracks. "I'm sorry, that's not really anything to do with you."

"You should stop apologising for the things

you've never been told," I tell her. "And maybe I can help with that too. You can ask me anything you want, and I'll answer, no judgement."

"Even if it's embarrassing?"

"Especially then," I assure her. "And we don't have to do it in the water either, if you don't want. We can go for dinner or something."

"Like a date?" Her cheeks flame red. "I'm so...no. I'm not supposed to be sorry."

I chuckle. "If you aren't sorry, does that mean you're trying to ask me on a date?"

"I'm not very good at this," she mumbles.

I clear my throat. "Hey, Fiona, I have a question."

She gives me a quizzical look. "Yes?"

"Will you go out to dinner with me? As a date."

"Are you serious?"

I nod. "Or we can just pretend that we haven't had this conversation and go back to swimming lessons," I add quickly in case she feels too pressured by the situation.

"I think I'd like a date," she says softly. "I've never been this forward before."

"Me neither," I admit. "And if you hadn't brought it up first, I'd probably have spent our next five lessons trying to find some way to."

Her whole face lights up at my admission. "Is that why you agreed to help me?"

"I don't know." I'm not going to lie to her about it, especially not when she's been so honest with me about all of the mer stuff so far. "It wasn't a very thought-through agreement."

"Nor from me," she agrees. "I just blurted out that I couldn't swim like I've told everyone. Which I haven't. I've been too embarrassed."

"I'm glad you told me. And that you trust me to help. Now, are you ready to go a bit deeper?"

"I'll still be able to sit at the bottom of the pool?" she asks.

I nod.

"Okay. Let's go deeper." She's barely finished saying it when she shuffles through the water. It takes me a moment to realise she's moving that way because she doesn't know the alternatives.

Not wanting to make her feel self-conscious about it, I shuffle myself deeper in the same way.

It's clear she's going to need a lot of time to become confident in the water, but I don't mind. If anything, I'm looking forward to seeing someone as brave as this flourish, and I'm honoured she's going to let me be part of her journey.

And I'm looking forward to getting to go on a date.

FIVE

Fiona

I'M EXHAUSTED by the time I get back to my flat, but in a good way. I'm not sure what I expected from a first swimming lesson, but it certainly wasn't talking for most of it. I know some people might question whether that was actually useful, but I do feel like it helped me be more at ease in the water.

I guess the question is going to be how I feel next time I'm near the pool.

I head to the kitchen to make myself a drink, surprised to find Bernie standing in front of the fridge with a dissatisfied expression on her face.

"You okay?" I ask.

"Oh, sorry, I didn't realise anyone was here," she says as she turns to face me. "I'm trying to pluck up the courage to drink blood."

"I thought things were better since Shane helped you with the blood thing?"

She sighs. "They are. But I still struggle with the idea of it. I know drinking blood is an important part of being a vampire, but I just don't get it. You know? Sorry, no, you don't know."

"Actually, I kind of do," I admit.

She frowns and waits for me to elaborate.

I grab the kettle in an attempt to keep myself busy so I don't overthink what I'm about to say.

"I don't know if Mickie told you, but I don't know how to swim."

"But you're a mermaid," she counters.

"Which is everyone's response. I'm a mermaid who can't swim. I get seasick too, so I understand a thing or two about having something that's supposed to be part of you that doesn't quite feel right." I fill up the kettle, trying to ignore the way my heart is pounding at saying it out loud.

"I didn't even realise that was possible."

"I don't think it is for born mer," I respond. "But I never learned to swim when I was human, so it stands to reason I can't swim now." I flick the button to start the water boiling.

"I didn't realise."

"I haven't really talked about it before," I admit. "At least, not until the past few days. I'm not sure what's changed."

She shrugs. "That one's easy. You've become more at ease with having a supernatural part of yourself and now you're starting to explore it more."

"Is that how you feel?" I gesture for her to hand me her mug, which she grabs from her cupboard.

I start making us drinks, only half-surprised to realise I know what she likes.

"I've never thought about it that way until I just said it, but I think so." She heads over to the table and sits down. "I don't know what it's like for you, but I try not to think about the night I became this."

"I don't either," I agree. "Though it was day for me."

"What happened?"

"The same as any turned mer. I drowned."

Bernie winces. "I'm sorry, that's awful."

"It was." I touch my throat, almost feeling the burn all over again. "But the sea is merciful as well as cruel, and here I am. What about you?" I wouldn't normally ask, but it seems as if this is the time to. And honestly, it feels good to talk about.

"I was on the way back from my boyfriend's house and I was attacked. All I really remember is the terror and feeling really faint. The blood loss affected me really quickly and the next thing I knew, I was scared of the sun." A tear rolls down her cheek.

"I'm sorry."

She smiles weakly. "Don't be. It wasn't your fault any more than it was mine. Or vampire-kind in general. Most of them don't go around attacking people despite the propaganda the vampire hunting guild used to put out."

"I've never seen any of that." I pick up the kettle and pour water over our tea bags.

"It's no longer in business, something about an explosion a few years back. I only know about it because of the vampire history lessons I've been taking," she says.

I take our mugs over to the table along with the bottle of milk so we don't have to go back and forth.

"How long ago was it that you were turned?" I ask.

"It was about eighteen months ago. I had everything lined up to go to university to study medicine, and then this happened. I had to drop out of the course I was going to be on, which is how I ended up coming here instead."

"I didn't realise you couldn't become a doctor if

you're a vampire." I wrap my hands around my mug and enjoy the warmth seeping through it.

"You can. I'm just not sure if it's right for me anymore."

"You have a long life ahead of you to decide, though," I point out.

"True. But I wasn't in a position to go anyway. My boyfriend broke up with me because he wasn't happy that he only got to see me at night."

"But..."

She gives a small laugh and holds up a hand to stop me in my tracks. "I know. But I see that one as a narrow escape for me. If it wasn't this, then it would have been something else down the road."

"That's a good way of looking at it."

"I think so," Bernie agrees. "It took me a while, but I'm in a much better position now I'm here at the academy than I was last year. I've met all you guys, and Shane. The only thing I need to get over is my blood aversion, but even that's better than it was."

"I'm glad."

"So that's me. What about you?"

"What about me?" I fish out my tea bag and add a dash of milk to my tea.

"Well I just shared my turning story, it's time for you to tell yours."

"Oh, right." Somehow, I managed to forget that's what we're doing while my heart broke for her. "It was eight years ago for me. I was on holiday with my parents and brother when it happened. It was an interesting experience going through the changes."

"When did you figure out you were mer?"

"It was fairly obvious when I woke up on the beach with a tail," I admit. "Though my hair turning green was a close second. I actually thought it was because I'd swallowed too much seaweed at first."

Bernie chuckles. "I can see how that would make sense to a ten-year-old."

"I didn't have anyone to explain these things to me. My parents refused to talk about everything that happened. I'm not sure if it's because they feel guilty, or because of how bad they felt when they thought I was gone, but it's just not something we've ever talked about."

"What about your brother?"

"He'd only just turned seven, I'm not sure he even remembers it."

"So what made you come here?"

"Mum, actually. We've never talked about the accident, but when it came time to pick my further education, she suggested I look into Obscure Academy and here I am. Finally learning a lot of the things that would have been helpful years ago."

"Including how to swim?"

"They do say better late than never, right?"

"I suppose that's true for both of us. Especially after being given a second chance at life."

I lean back in my chair and consider her words for a moment. "I've never thought about it like that before."

"It was one of the things I saw suggested online when I looked up how to deal with being turned," Bernie responds. "Apparently, the outlook doesn't work for everyone, but many turned vampires can get some peace from it. Maybe you can too?"

I nod but don't say anything. I'm not sure there's anything *to* say.

"But wow, that was draining," she jokes. "I think the blood will be a welcome distraction now."

"I'm sorry."

"Don't be. Sometimes it's good for us to talk about these things," she reminds me. "It's easy to ignore the things that traumatised us, but we can't ignore them forever."

"I'm starting to realise that."

"The swimming?"

I nod. "I've been scared of going back in the water."

"Understandable."

"But also problematic when I'm part fish."

A loud laugh bursts from her and she covers her mouth quickly. "I'm sorry, it's just when you said it like that it sounded funny."

I join her amusement, seeing exactly what she means. "Well, it's true. I am part fish. And it's time I did something for that part of me."

"What's changed?"

My cheeks flush.

"Ah, the someone we were teasing you about last night."

I open my mouth to argue, then shut it again. "All right, yes. But we haven't even been on a date yet, so it might not be anything."

"Mmhmm. Do they have a name?"

"He does."

"But you're not going to tell me it, are you?" Bernie guesses.

"He's called Wade," I say. "But we're still getting to know each other, so it might not be anything. We're going on a date on Monday."

"A date is good," Bernie says. "Though Monday is an interesting choice."

I shrug. "It's as good as any other day."

"True." Her phone starts vibrating and she lets out a groan. "Time for me to get to class. I guess that means the blood can't wait any longer."

"Oh, right. I forgot your classes haven't started yet."

"One of the perks of being a vampire. It's a good job I was never a morning person or I'd really struggle."

"Surely this is just your morning now?" I ask.

"I'm not actually sure," she admits. "Sometimes, I feel like it is. Others, it just feels like evening, especially when people are going about their days without me."

I nod but don't say how much I think it must suck to have to miss as much of the day as vampires have to. I don't think Bernie will appreciate the reminder.

"I'll see you later," she says, getting to her feet.

"See you." I head off to my room, my head racing to think through everything we touched on in our conversation.

Regardless of the reasons, I'm finally ready to face what it means to be mer, and I'm looking forward to learning more about myself in the process.

SIX

FIONA

WHAT AM I doing and why do I think this is a good idea? Wade is supposed to be teaching me how to swim, not going out for dinner with me.

I look up at the sign hanging above the restaurant and let out a small laugh. He's asked me out for sushi of all things.

"Something amusing?" Wade asks from beside me, the amused grin on his face revealing that he probably knows exactly why I'm laughing.

"I didn't think you'd want to eat fish. Aren't they your friends or something?"

"Have you ever known a cow shifter?" he returns.

"Yes." Where is he going with this?

"But you still eat beef, right?"

"Yes."

"Then why wouldn't I eat fish?" He cocks his head to the side and studies me as he waits for my answer.

"When you put it like that, it makes a lot of sense," I admit.

"Have you been avoiding eating fish since you turned mer?" he asks.

A furious blush rushes to my cheeks. "Yes."

"We can go somewhere else, if you want?" he offers quickly.

I shake my head. "I love fish. I've just been avoiding it because I thought it was wrong for me to eat them."

"In which case, I'm glad I can be the one to tell you that it's not taboo. Most merfolk eat fish."

"Then I have a lot of meals to make up on."

He chuckles. "Shall we?" He gestures to the door and guides me inside with a hand hovering by the small of my back but not quite touching.

I wish he would, but it's too early for that.

Cool air greets us the moment we step into the restaurant, followed by an overly friendly woman whose smile doesn't reach her eyes. Either she's having a bad day, or she just hates her job.

"I have a reservation," Wade says. "Under Fisher."

I quirk an eyebrow, surprised by the name.

"Follow me," the woman says, leading us over to a booth at the back. "The specials are on the board over there." She waves in the vague direction, then disappears, leaving the two of us alone.

I shuffle into the booth, pleasantly surprised to find there's plenty of room without destroying the intimacy of the setting.

"You said I could ask you anything, right?" I check.

"You can," he promises. "What's on your mind?"

"Fisher?" I ask.

Wade chuckles. "I should have guessed. It's a common mer name. Up until we came out into the open, we didn't have surnames, so a lot of people just adopted common human surnames that have something to do with fish or the sea. You'll find a lot of Basses and Codds too."

"I'll add it to the list of things I had no idea about. Maybe I need to start carrying a notepad around with me."

"Then consider me your guide to all things mer."

He gives me a small mock bow, bringing a smile to my face.

"You might need to be my guide to all things sushi." I stare at the menu, trying to make sense of the different terms.

"What kind of thing do you like?"

"I have no idea, I haven't eaten fish since I was ten. I wasn't exactly into sushi then."

"Ah, so that's when you turned mer."

"Yes." I can tell that he's curious about it but he's not willing to press me on the details yet. Maybe that will come in time.

And maybe I'll end up wanting to tell him.

"We could get one of the set menus and share?" he suggests.

"I'm good with that." I'm not sure what it is about his suggestion that really drives it home that we're on a proper date, but the realisation has only just come over me.

"Then we're going to use my favourite method to decide between them," he says.

I shoot him a curious look, trying to work out what he has planned.

To my surprise, he pulls out a coin. "Heads or tails?"

"Tails."

"All right, if it lands on tails, we'll have menu A,

if it's heads, we'll order menu B." He balances the coin on his thumb and flicks it into the air with ease.

It lands on the table and comes to a stop. I reach out and pull it to me. "Tails, I think. What coin is this?"

"It's a Merton coin," Wade responds. "They're not used very much anymore, but I always like to carry one for situations like this. You can keep it, if you want."

"Are you sure?"

He nods.

"Thank you."

"It's not worth much, if that's what you're thinking."

I turn the coin over in my hands, noticing that the other side of it seems to have a fish head on it. It's nothing like the coins I'm used to. "I wasn't," I admit. "I've just never seen anything like it."

"Is menu A okay?" Wade checks.

"Isn't it what the coin said we're supposed to have?"

"Yes, but we can overrule the coin."

"Then what's the point of it?" I ask, running my finger over the engraved fish head.

"An icebreaker, perhaps."

I smile reassuringly at him. "Menu A is good

with me," I promise. "And some water, unless there's a drink I should be having instead."

"Water is good." He reaches out and takes the menu from me, letting our fingers brush against one another as he does.

From the look on his face, he knows what he's doing and it makes the touch even more electric than before.

I clear my throat to rid myself of the daze that's fallen over me. "You never did tell me what kind of fish your tail is," I point out.

"You're right, I got distracted. It's a striped bass tail."

"Oh, that's cool."

"You have no idea what one looks like, do you?" he asks.

"It looks like your tail, but with a fish head."

He lets out a surprised laugh. "I fell for that one, didn't I?"

A wide smile spreads over my face. "A little bit, yes."

A waiter appears, cutting off our conversation, though I'm grateful we're not being served by the woman who greeted us originally. Wade orders for us and the man disappears to deal with our drinks.

"So, what else do you want to know?" he asks.

"This is a proper date, right?"

"I'd like it to be," he responds. "Why?"

"It's just that I feel like we've talked a lot about me and I want to get to know you too. It's fun learning all the new things about merfolk, but what about you specifically?" I tuck a strand of hair behind my ear and rest my chin on my hand while I wait for him to answer.

"Do you have anything specific you want to know?" he asks.

"I don't know. Do you have any siblings?"

He nods. "Two brothers, they're both older than me. One lives in Merton and the other lives in a mer settlement in France."

"France?"

"He did a French exchange program when he was at school and met a French girl. No one thought it would last, but he moved to France to be with her as soon as he'd finished with his education and they've been married for three years."

"That's sweet."

"He definitely thinks so," Wade agrees. "What about you?"

"I have a brother. He's fifteen now and decidedly human. We're not very close."

"Because you're mer?"

I frown. "I've never thought about it, but maybe? I suppose it must be strange for him to have a supernatural sister, while I sometimes wished that I could be as human as him." The past week has been full of revelations about how I feel about things in reality. "Did you have any pets as a kid?"

"No. But I did make friends with a stingray once."

"What? That's so cool. I have to hear more about that." I lean closer to him, wanting to catch every word.

"I think it was lost. I met him while we were on holiday off the coast of Spain a few years ago. I'd swim with him every day and he never ran away."

"Have you ever seen a shark?"

"Of course."

"Outside of an aquarium."

He chuckles. "Yes, outside of an aquarium."

"What was it like?"

"It depends on the shark. The small ones are just fun to watch, and the basking sharks are awe-inspiring in size, but they're gentle giants. Great whites and tiger sharks on the other hand..." A shiver runs down his spine. "I kept thinking they were going to eat me. Mer look even more like seals than humans in wetsuits."

"I'll keep that in mind if I ever find myself in close proximity to one."

"You really should. They've been known to attack merfolk."

"I feel like that was a bad topic choice," I admit.

"Not at all. I love the sea."

"What's the best thing you've seen in it?" My curiosity gets the better of me even if I've never thought about the ocean in a particularly positive way.

"A sea turtle over a reef," he says with certainty. "Nothing can describe how that looked, it's something you have to experience for yourself."

"I probably have a long way to go before that's possible," I admit.

"You might surprise yourself. You did well on Friday."

"All we did was sit and talk," I point out.

Two glasses of water and a bowl of edamame beans are set down between us, but our waiter doesn't say anything and disappears to the kitchen.

I pick up my chopsticks and use them to grab one of the beans and pop it into my mouth.

"Did you really expect to swim on the first day?" Wade asks.

I frown as I consider the point behind his question. "I'm not sure what I expected."

"The fact you stayed in the water the whole time

and didn't freak out is a great start. But we can do more in the next lesson if you think you're ready?"

"I don't know if I am. But there's only one way to find out. I definitely feel less intimidated than I did before, you really put me at ease. Thank you."

His whole face lights up at the compliment. "You're welcome."

More of our food arrives and our conversation turns to more mundane topics, but it isn't lost on me how easy I find it to talk to him, or how close we're sitting together.

I hope he feels the same way, because if he doesn't, then I may be heading towards heartbreak.

SEVEN

FIONA

AFTER A WEEK of almost daily lessons, walking into the pool house isn't as nerve-wracking as it used to be. I may even go as far as to say that I look forward to my sessions with Wade.

Though perhaps that's more to do with the company than anything else. Despite his hope that he'd be able to help me with the actual swimming, I haven't managed yet.

Perhaps today will be the day.

I push through the door and let the familiar tang of salt water fill my senses. The way the whole place makes me feel has definitely changed. It's less intimidating than before, and it makes me feel accomplished in a way I don't think I have before.

Wade hears me coming and turns around, his whole face lighting up when he sees me even though he knows I'm coming to meet him. "Hey."

"Hi."

"Ready for your next lesson?"

I nod. "I hope your other students aren't too annoyed that I'm taking up all your time at the moment."

"Your lessons are coming out of my free hours," he promises. "No one knows a thing."

"Ah, so that's why we're here daily."

He nods. "It's my very transparent plan to spend more time with you."

"You know you could just ask me on another date," I point out.

"True. But there are other people there."

He has a point. One of the things that's nice about our lessons is that it's just the two of us and the pool.

I make my way to the edge of it, my gaze fixated on the water lapping at the edge.

I reach down and pull my dress over my head, dropping it to the side, surprising myself with the motion as I've never done it before. But I can feel how much my clothes have been restricting me while I'm in the pool, and even if I feel exposed like this, I'm not technically naked by mer standards. A light sheen of scales spreads from my knees, all the way up to my collar bones. I can make them go away if I think about it, but I've never really seen the need to.

I glance at Wade, who seems as surprised as I am by my choice, but he doesn't say anything and grabs his own shirt, pulling it over his head and giving me another glimpse of his chest. His scales don't travel up quite as far as mine and don't do anything to hide his swimmer's physique. I haven't spent enough time examining other merfolk bodies to know whether it's natural or because of his profession, and I'm not brave enough to ask, especially when we've only been on one date and we haven't even kissed yet. I keep thinking I want to make that move and then backing out at the last moment.

"Shall we?" he gestures to the water.

I nod and sit down on the side of the pool, dangling my legs in and letting the urge to change come over me. In the blink of an eye, my legs are replaced by a tail. Taking a deep breath, I ease myself down into the water, going a little deeper than the first time.

I pause, waiting for the panic to set in, but it doesn't.

"What now?" I ask Wade.

"I'm guessing you don't know how to tread water in your human form?"

"What's that?"

"Something that probably won't ever matter to you," he answers honestly. "I thought we could start simple and teach you how to keep yourself floating with your head above water, that way you don't have to worry about holding your breath."

"I can't breathe underwater?"

"No. You're a mammal."

"Huh. I just assumed that we breathed like fish do in this form."

He raises an eyebrow. "We don't have gills."

"And now you say that, it makes sense, but it's not something I've ever had to test."

"That's fair," he says. "Why don't you come grab hold of me?" he suggests.

"Okay, but why?"

"I'm going to take us deeper so I can teach you what to do, but you'll need help."

There's a bit of distance between us, but I use what he's taught me already to propel myself in his direction using my tail to move. It's a weird sensation, but rewarding at the same time. I'd never have been able to do this a few weeks ago.

I reach him and come to a rest. My fins flick back and forth almost as if they have a mind of their own. I put my arms on his shoulders, only realising after I do how close it brings us.

We don't say a word, nor do we move beyond what's needed in the water. Everything is just...still.

He places a hand on my waist just above where my tail starts. The scales there are sensitive and I can feel his touch as well as if it was my bare skin.

His gaze flicks to my lips and my breathing hitches as I realise what's about to happen.

And it's what I've been hoping for.

I'm not sure which of us moves first, but my arms tighten around his neck as he pulls me closer with a hand on the small of my back. I'm dimly aware of our tails brushing against one another as our lips meet and my eyes flutter closed.

Nothing matters other than our kiss and the way it feels for the two of us to connect like this.

We break apart, but he doesn't let go of me. I meet his gaze, seeing a lot of the same emotions I'm feeling in his eyes.

"I've been thinking about that since our date," Wade whispers.

"Me too," I admit. I bite my bottom lip, drawing his attention to it.

"Though it wasn't quite what I had in mind for today's lesson," he admits.

"How long do we have the pool for?"

"Another hour or so."

"Oh good." I swish my hand through the water, almost amazed that the fact I'm sitting in it hasn't taken anything away from our kiss. I've spent so long scared of water because of the bad memories I've associated with it.

But now I have a good one. And I'm going to use it to push back the residual fear resting inside me. If something as perfect as my first kiss with Wade can happen in the water, then it can't be too bad, can it?

"I think I'm ready to try swimming," I say.

He frowns. "That's not quite the response I expected."

I let out a small laugh, feeling freer from my fear of the water than I have in a long time. "Trust me?"

"I think I'm the one who's supposed to say that." His voice is light and inquisitive.

"You told me that I should have some instincts for it, right?"

"For swimming? In theory, yes. I think your feelings about the water were blocking them."

"Okay. Fish me out if it all goes wrong?" I ask.

He looks as if he's about to argue, but I don't let him. Instead, I take a deep breath and drop myself under the water.

I freeze, wondering what I'm doing and why I'm being so reckless, but then something takes over that I haven't experienced before. I recall the movements Wade has been teaching me over the past week and flick my tail.

I move forward, pulling myself with my arms. It isn't graceful, and I realise it's going to take more practice to get it right, but I think what I'm doing is swimming.

My lungs start to burn and I head back to the surface, breaking through with a splash and gasp in another lungful of air.

Wade makes his way over quickly and puts himself within touching distance.

"I did it!"

"You did." He smiles at me, clearly impressed.

"Thank you," I say.

"For what?"

"For teaching me."

"Apparently you didn't need me at all," he jokes, but I can tell he's not upset by it.

"That's not true," I counter, moving closer to him.

He reaches out and meets me partway. "Well, I'm glad either way."

Even though I can't touch the bottom of the pool, I feel perfectly safe in his arms, and give myself over to a second kiss.

If I'd known this was how learning to swim would go, maybe I'd have tried to learn earlier.

Then again, I'm not sure just any teacher would have been able to get me this far. And hopefully, Wade will decide that I still have lots to learn so we can spend more time here.

I can't think of anything better.

EIGHT

WADE

I CHECK my phone as I enter the swimming pool, hoping that I'm not going to find a message from Fiona saying that she needs to cancel. I don't see why she would, but a small part of me is worrying since this is the first time we've been to the pool since we kissed.

What if she thinks I expect it to happen again?

I mean, there's a part of me that hopes it does, but I don't want her to feel pressured.

To my relief, there's nothing from her, though there is an email from my English Lit professor.

Confused, I click it open, my heart sinking as I read it.

"Hey," Fiona says brightly as she approaches.

I look up in time to see her face falling.

"What's wrong?" she asks, reaching out as if she's going to touch me, only to let her hand fall back down, unsure whether it's a good idea.

I close my eyes and let out a deep breath. "It's nothing to worry about."

"Okay."

I open my eyes again, admittedly confused.

"What? If you wanted to tell me, then you would, if you don't, then I have to assume you have a good reason," Fiona responds. "Unless it's that you have a girlfriend."

I chuckle dryly. "I don't have a girlfriend."

"Good. Then I can ask you on another date."

"I'd like that."

"All right, time to swim?"

Is it me, or does she seem excited about the prospect? It's only a few weeks ago that she was scared to spend any time in the water, now she's eager to. It's amazing how much progress she's made. She's shared such a vulnerable part of herself with me.

And then there's me not telling her about an email.

"I failed an English paper," I admit.

She blinks a few times. "What?"

"You asked what was wrong. I just got an email from my professor saying that he can't accept my paper because it doesn't meet the minimum grades."

"Oh, Wade, I'm sorry. What's it on?"

"Symbolism in Hamlet." I groan and run my hand over my face, trying not to let the frustration overcome me. "I just don't seem to understand it."

Her face lights up. "Then it's perfect."

I cock my head to the side, more than a little confused by her seeming excitement about the situation. "I'm not sure I follow."

"My last English paper in school was on that, my teacher loved Shakespeare so it was actually kind of fun. I know it's not academy level, but maybe I can help you with it?" She reaches out and places a hand on my arm. "I don't have to help if you don't want, but I'd be happy to."

"Are you sure?"

She smiles up at me. "Absolutely. You're helping me with something I'm not good at, let me help you with something you aren't," she says.

"When you put it like that, you're hard to resist."

Her lips quirk up into a smile. "I'd hope I'm hard to resist anyway." She steps back, taking herself closer to the pool. She starts undoing the buttons of her shirt, and even though I know it's perfectly normal for mer to strip off in front of one another, I can't help but feel like this is something more.

"If you're willing to help, I'd like that," I say before I completely lose focus on the conversation we're supposed to be having.

"I'm free after our swim. We could go for coffee and talk about Shakespeare. Or if you're hungry, we could grab a takeaway and head back to your flat."

I raise an eyebrow. "Not a restaurant?"

Fiona tucks a strand of shimmering green hair behind her ear. "There'd be too many people there."

"There'd be people around if we went for coffee too."

"You're right. I guess we're going back to your flat then." She drops her shirt to the side and starts working on the rest of her clothes, revealing the gorgeous green scales that cover the main part of her body, spreading up to her throat where they fade away into her skin.

"It sounds like a date."

She beams and sits on the edge of the pool. Her legs transform into a beautiful tail within moments, and the scales on her upper body darken to match the colour of her hair. I've seen plenty of mer transform before, but for some reason, I've never fully appreciated how beautiful the entire process is.

"Are you coming to join me?" she asks. "I know I can technically swim now, but I'd rather not get in on my own." A hint of vulnerability enters her voice, shaking me out of my thoughts.

"Sorry." I strip off my shirt and swim shorts and head over to join her, enjoying the way she watches me as I do. I suppose growing up human means that she'll have a different view on whether it's appropriate for us to just take our clothes off like this.

I sit down next to her and let my tail spring forth.

"Can I touch it?" Fiona asks.

I raise an eyebrow. "You want to touch my tail?"

A blush rushes over her cheeks. "I've never touched a mer-tail that isn't my own before," she admits. "At least not on purpose. Brushing past it in the pool doesn't seem to count."

"If you want, but..." I trail off.

"But?"

"Well, I guess keep in mind where my legs would be."

Her blush deepens. "I don't have to..."

I reach out and take her hand in mine, moving it so that she touches the point on my waist where my tail begins.

Fiona shuffles closer, her fingers drifting across

my scales. Her touch is gentle, but that only makes me *more* aware of it, and not less.

"They're soft."

"So are yours," I point out, remembering how it felt to touch them when I kissed her.

"But they're different from mine."

"That's because we have different tails," I point out. "They'll all be similar in a lot of ways, but they still feel different."

"Right, it all depends."

I nod. "Precisely."

"It's a lot to learn," she admits. "I thought swimming was the big thing I was missing, but that's not true, is it?"

"I think you're doing fine."

"I might be, but there's still so much I don't understand about being mer. I don't even know the differences between the different types of merfolk."

"I don't think anyone knows that," I assure her. "Think about how vast the seas are, for all we know, there are hundreds of subspecies of merfolk that haven't been discovered yet."

Her eyes widen. "Hundreds?"

"Maybe that's unlikely," I correct myself. "But there's going to be at least one. Merfolk were late to join the rest of the supernatural out in the open."

"I've always wondered why."

"Simple, most of them live in the sea. A lot didn't hear about it, and if they did, they saw no real benefit in joining everyone else on land. It's only in the past hundred years or so that we've ventured onto land more. And then there's the fact that humans somehow believed in mer at the same time as dismissing all stories about them as fiction."

"Like the Little Mermaid," she half-jokes.

"Yep, exactly like her."

"Wait, the story is real?"

"I'm not sure if real is the right word. It's one of those stories that's been twisted a lot from how it really happened. But she was a real person, yes."

"Huh." She swishes her hand through the water. "I guess I never thought about whether some of the old folk tales might just have been caused by supernaturals."

"Not all of them were. I don't see how it would be possible for a witch to decide to eat children."

"Or make a house out of sweets in the first place. Surely it would disintegrate the first time it rained?"

I laugh. "Maybe, but if it's made by magic, I'm sure there'd be a weather-proofing spell on it."

"Hmm, good point." She glances at the clock on the wall. "We're wasting our swimming time. I need the practice."

"We can swim now and continue the conversation over dinner?" I suggest.

"That sounds good to me." She slips into the water.

I watch intently as she leans back, using her tail to keep herself steady like I've shown her to. Her hair floats around her, giving her an ethereal look that transports me straight back to the sea.

I've never understood what the human fascination with the beauty of merfolk is until this moment. Seeing her like this in the water, it all becomes clear to me where it's come from.

I push the thoughts to the side and get into the pool myself. She still has a lot of swimming practice she needs to do before she can even think about going in the open water, but she's doing well, and I want to help with that in any way I can.

And if that means I get to spend more time with her in the process, then that's a good thing.

NINE

FIONA

I SIT on the side of the pool and swish my legs back and forth. My skin tingles as the urge to let out my tail grows within me. If I was just here alone with Wade, it would already be out, but there are so many people about during the MerSoc meeting that I'm not sure how I feel about it.

"Hey, Fi," Melody says as she takes a seat next to me and dips her legs into the pool.

"I didn't realise you'd arrived," I say to my friend.

"I came changed." She gestures to the bikini she's wearing. As difficult as it's been for me to get my tail out, it must be so much worse for her in that she can't do it at all unless she risks enchanting all of the non-sirens in the room.

"How did meeting Josh's parents go? You never said."

Her eyes light up. "It went well. Or at least, I think it did. His mum was a little wary at first, but she relaxed when she realised I knew how to sign."

I frown. "Didn't Josh already tell her you could?"

"He did, but she's very protective of him."

"Understandably. I can imagine it must be terrifying to her."

Melody chuckles. "Don't say that around Josh, he'll give you a lecture about how he's perfectly capable of looking after himself. Which he is. But I do get it. There's a lot more to think about than I expected when we started dating."

I nod. I can't pretend to understand, but I know she's put a lot of work into making sure she can accommodate Josh's deafness.

"But he's worth it." She lets out a sigh.

A splash in the water diverts our conversation away from the topic at hand and Georgie pops her head out of the water. She makes the rest of the way over and hoists herself up onto the side.

"You have a serious expression on your face," Melody says. "What are you planning?"

"You haven't got us involved in another party, have you?" I add.

Georgie chuckles. "Not until next Christmas. You know we'll be organising the Christmas Pool Party every year now."

"How long are you planning on staying at Obscure Academy?" I ask.

"At least two more years," she responds. "My course is four. And that's if I don't do a Master's afterwards."

"She's never leaving," Melody quips.

Georgie rolls her eyes. "I will. But no, it's not about a party, it's about the Merton visit. Helena wants final numbers so she knows how much to charge each of us for the bus. Are you coming?"

Melody shakes her head. "I haven't experimented enough with my magic reserves to be able to guarantee I can have my tail out long enough."

Georgie nods. "I thought as much, though maybe you'll be able to next year?"

"I hope so," the siren responds. "At least it's a possibility now. Josh is helping me experiment more."

A smile spreads over my face at hearing the

happiness in her voice. It must have been really hard not to sing when she loves it, but since discovering that Josh can't be affected by her voice, and even seems to enjoy it when she sings, she's been even brighter than before.

"What about you?" Georgie asks. "Are you coming to Merton?"

I glance across the pool to where Wade is talking to some of the others. He notices me watching and flashes a smile in my direction. I return it, feeling a fluttering in my chest at the interaction. "Mmhmm."

Georgie follows my gaze and lets out an amused snort. "I see you hit it off with Wade, then."

A blush spreads over my cheeks. "You knew I would when you left me alone to meet him." I'm not sure how well they know one another, but they seem to have at least some kind of knowledge about each other.

"So you're coming to Merton because of Wade?" Georgie asks.

"In a way." If it wasn't for him, I wouldn't be able to go. I suspect that probably counts as going because of him. "But I've also never been."

"Right, you're turned," she says, nodding along. "Sometimes I forget."

"I suppose there's no reason to really think about it," I say. "You didn't know me when I was human."

"What colour was your hair?" she asks.

"What?" I reach up and touch it.

"Before you were turned. I don't imagine your hair was always green."

I chuckle. "No, it wasn't. I was blonde." It seems like so long ago now that I only really think about it when I see photos from my childhood. "I think this suits me better."

Georgie leans back and squints. "Yeah, I can't imagine you blonde, sorry."

"Maybe you'd have ended up dying it a different colour," Melody says.

"I did always love seeing photos of people with lots of different colours in their hair," I muse. "I begged Mum to let me do it at one point, but she said no. I guess she lost the argument in a different way."

"Maybe you just always knew that you were destined to be mer," Georgie says.

"I don't think that's how it works." Though it could be. Considering the process involves the discomfort of drowning, I doubt there are people around who are willing to become mer as an experiment.

"Oh, but if you're coming to Merton, that means I'm finally going to see your tail," Georgie says.

I chuckle. "You're very excited about that."

"Ever since you told me that it's a flying fish tail, I've wanted to see it. I've never seen one in person and I imagine it's beautiful."

That's not the reason I expected from her, but it makes me a lot less reluctant to actually reveal it.

Without any warning, I give in to the urge to let my tail free. I immediately feel the difference between the water on skin, and the water on my scales. It's soothing in a different way.

Georgie gasps.

"It's beautiful," Melody says.

"Thank you." I swish my tail through the water, enjoying the sensation.

A splash at the other side of the pool calls my attention and I look up in time to see the deep green of Wade's tail disappear under the surface.

My heart skips a beat as my gaze locks onto where he's swimming across the pool towards me. He must have noticed me releasing my tail and want to make sure I'm comfortable.

As I suspected, his head pops up out of the water a few feet away.

"I think that's our cue to leave, Mel," Georgie says.

"Hey, G," Wade says.

"Hurt her, and I'll hurt you," my friend responds.

Wade chuckles. "I'll let you."

"Good."

I shake my head in bemusement. I strip off my shirt and slip into the water, trying to ignore the nerves building inside me over the fact I'm about to swim in front of others. It's one thing for Wade to know, but the others are different.

But if I'm going to go with them to Merton, that's going to happen anyway.

I make my way over to him, coming to a stop in the water and flicking my tail in order to hover in place. He reaches out under the water to put a hand on my waist, though I don't know if it's because he wants to touch me, or if he wants to make sure he's supporting me.

"You got your tail out," he says softly.

I nod. "Georgie keeps asking me about it, and if I want to go to Merton, then everyone's going to see it anyway. Unless you don't think I can swim well enough for the trip..." I should have thought about that part of it, but for some reason, it didn't cross my mind.

"You're the only person who can know if you're ready," he tells me. "But you don't have to do it alone. I'll be there."

"That does make me feel a lot better," I say, reaching up and touching his cheek.

I want to kiss him, but I'm not sure if it's appropriate in front of people.

Wade's lips quirk up into a smile and his eyes soften as he looks at me. "If you want to, I'm okay with it."

"What?"

"You're thinking about kissing me."

"How can you tell that?"

"Because of the way you're looking at me," he responds.

"You don't mind? Even though we're in front of everyone?"

"I don't think any of them are paying attention," he points out. "And even if they are, I don't see why it would be a problem to announce to everyone that I'm dating the most beautiful mermaid at the academy."

My cheeks flush and I let out a snort of bemusement. "I'm sure I'm not the *most* beautiful."

"You are to me." He leans in and presses his lips against mine.

I wrap my arms around his neck and kiss him back, not caring about anything or anyone else.

We break apart and I smile up at him, feeling as if we're in a world of our own. "I'm looking forward to seeing Merton," I admit. "It's where you grew up, right?"

He nods. "And I'm going to show you all my favourite places from when I was a kid."

"I like the sound of that." The swimming part has me a little worried, but I want to see the underwater city where a lot of the mer live, it sounds like something out of a movie.

And if it means more time with Wade, then that's a bonus.

TEN

Fiona

I EAT my soup and send a few messages back and forth to one of my coursework groups. Our final presentation is in a few days and I know they want to get things straightened out. I wish I didn't have this to take my attention away from the other things going on in my life.

Like kissing Wade. And dating Wade.

Eurgh, why am I becoming like this? I've never felt this way about someone before, and it's leaving me surprisingly confused by the whole situation. And not at the same time. It really does seem simple in some ways. I like Wade, he seems to like me, and that's that.

I'm not about to let it distract me from my academy work or my ambitions, but that also doesn't mean I should let it pass me by.

The door slams open and Michaela stumbles inside with dark smudges on her cheeks and on her glasses.

"Mickie, what happened?" I ask, dropping my phone on the table and jumping to my feet. I point to one of the chairs and make her sit.

She lets out a loud sigh. "Potions."

I shake my head in bewilderment as I make my way over to the kettle to make her a drink. Though perhaps she needs something a bit stronger.

"I thought you were trying to avoid potions?"

She sighs. "It was an accident."

"I guessed that much." I take the mug of tea I've made her and set it down in front of her. "Want to talk about it?"

"I tried to make a hangover cure."

"So is the tea the wrong thing to make? I don't have any coke left, but I think I saw some of Bernie's tomato juice in the fridge, she won't mind if we use it."

Mickie groans. "I'm not drinking a Bloody Mary. I don't know how she stands them."

"Let's face it, that's not the weirdest thing Bernie drinks."

"Hmm, true. I suppose tomato juice and vodka is much better than blood."

"I think Bernie agrees with you."

I grab some painkillers from my cupboard and hand them to the witch. "I know it's not as good as a magical hangover cure, but at least it's something."

"Thanks. Did your mer-tail trick work by the way? I forgot to ask you."

"It did. I'm definitely saving that one for next time I drink."

"Oh good." She pops out two of the painkillers and swallows them dry.

"Thank you for listening to me when I was having my little drunk shower," I say. "I really appreciate it."

"What are friends for? Drunken heart-to-hearts and painkillers the morning after seem right to me," Mickie jokes.

"I'd hope there'll be some sober heart-to-hearts in there too."

"Mmm. I hate that I can't make potions," Mickie says. "I know that I say I'm fine with it, but I'm not."

"Could you learn how?" I ask.

She shakes her head. "It's not like swimming. I

can't learn it because there's something missing in my magic."

"Are any of your other family members like that?"

"Not as far as I know, but it's not something we talk about often. Nobody ever wants to talk about it."

"I'm sorry."

She shrugs. "Don't be. I'm used to it."

"But you shouldn't have to be."

"Interesting that you say that when I know your family rarely talked about the fact you're a mermaid."

"Maybe that's exactly why I know you should talk about it," I respond.

"Hmm. True. But enough about me and my terrible potion making skills, you know plenty about them considering the flat pact."

"We're just trying to keep the kettle in one piece," I quip.

"I know, I know. Everyone wants me to stay away from the tea."

"I think it's more than everyone knows it'll be a disaster if there's no caffeine," I say.

A thoughtful expression crosses her face. "I have to admit, that sounds awful."

"It does."

She takes a sip of her tea and lets out a sigh. "Yep, I'd be sad if this went away."

"Then you should be glad the pact also involves making you tea."

"Oh, I am. How are things going with your merman by the way? Is that even the right way to describe him? I don't know much about merfolk."

"You can use merman," I respond. "At least, I think so. Though mer seems more commonly used."

"Because it's gender-neutral?"

"No idea, actually. There are a lot of gaps in my knowledge of mer. Which sucks considering I am one."

"Mmm, I can relate."

I nod, knowing she's telling the truth. Her issues with potions may come from a different place, but they still make her a little outside the ordinary for witches.

"They're going good, I think. We have a trip to Merton coming up, which will be nice. He grew up there, so he's going to show me around."

"Oh, that sounds fun. Where is it?"

"It's in the Humber estuary."

"*In* it?"

"In it, under it, I'm not really sure how to describe it. I honestly don't know what to expect at all."

"Something like out of a kids' show with mer?" Mickie suggests.

"Maybe? Though now I'm imagining large shell buildings, which doesn't seem likely. Or maybe it's just like up here but underwater."

"That doesn't seem likely," Michaela responds. "Wouldn't it be a problem with the salt?"

"I don't think estuaries are very salty." Though I won't pretend to know. I wasn't very good at paying attention to that part of my geography lessons in school, even if I should have been.

"Whatever it's like down there, you have got to tell me. And bring back photos if you can."

"I will," I promise, knowing that all of my friends will probably want to know what it's like, though my family probably won't care.

"Oh, has Krissi asked you about summer yet?"

"No?" At least, I don't think so.

"We're thinking of doing something, going to the beach, that kind of thing."

"That sounds cool," I admit, even if the beach is normally somewhere I've avoided. "Count me in."

"You don't need to check with your parents?"

I shrug. "I'm sure I'll talk to them about it before we book anything, but they won't mind." They'll probably like not having to look at me and remember what happened, but I don't say that part out loud.

"It's going to be fun," Mickie says. "I can't wait."

"Me neither." And it isn't a word of a lie. Spending some of the summer with the friends I've made at Obscure Academy sounds just perfect to me, even if the plans aren't completely set yet.

ELEVEN

FIONA

MY STOMACH TWISTS into knots as the bus speeds along the motorway and towards Merton. Now that I'm facing the idea of actually entering the water, I'm not so sure if it's a good idea or not.

Wade reaches out and takes my hand in his, giving it a squeeze. "You look like you need a distraction."

"I think I might," I respond. "I feel sick already."

"Oh, I'm glad you mentioned that."

I frown, confused by why that would be the case. He unzips his bag and pulls out a cardboard box, handing it to me.

"I remembered to grab them before we left. I wasn't sure if you'd already have some."

"Seasickness tablets," I say.

He nods. "You said you got seasick."

"I do. Or at least, I used to. I've done a lot of avoiding the sea since I turned."

"Understandably."

"I thought you said Merton was in the estuary."

"It is. But better safe than sorry, right?"

I nod.

"You should take one in about half an hour, that should make sure it kicks in by the time we're ready to get in the water."

"Thank you." My heart warms at the thought he put into getting them for me. It was only a passing comment in a bigger conversation, and it makes me feel like he listens to me. Not that I'm surprised by that given how well he taught me how to swim. I drop the box into my own bag. "How did your meeting with your English professor go?" I ask him, leaping on the chance to distract myself properly.

He grimaces. "Not as well as I wanted it to. Though he's said that if I can turn in a new paper by the end of next week, he'll overwrite the failing grade I've currently got."

"That's something, at least."

"Yeah. I'm not sure why I thought to take it as a module, I know I'm no good at this kind of thing."

"Then why did you?"

"You're asking good questions."

"I think that's normally what you're supposed to do when you're dating someone."

"I can think of other things we're supposed to do too," he quips.

"Wade!"

"What?" Mischief sparkles in his eyes.

"We're on a bus full of our friends."

He chuckles, a rich sound that goes right through me in the best way. "That's your problem with this conversation?"

"Should I have another one?"

He smoothes a thumb over the back of my hand. "I guess not. But we can save the conversation until we're alone."

I nod. "I like the sound of that. Though if this is your way of getting away from having a conversation about your module choices, you're wrong."

"It wasn't," he promises, then lets out a loud sigh. "I didn't know what I wanted to do when I came to Obscure Academy. I spent all of last year focusing on the subjects that sounded interesting to me, then realised that I needed to do something that would make me employable instead, so I recorrected and took a load of modules that I thought employers would like."

"That doesn't seem like a good reason to do anything."

"You're not wrong. At this rate, I'm just going to keep over-correcting and I'll be studying for the rest of my life."

"Or you'll become a swimming teacher properly," I say. "You're good at that."

"You've never seen me teaching."

"No, but I've experienced it. And maybe it was easier because my instincts should make it easier for me to swim, but I was also scared of the water."

"But you're not now?"

I glance out of the window, half expecting the sea to be there already. "I don't know. I'm trying to focus on Merton itself and not the water."

"You don't seem to have any problems at MerSoc."

"Now. You didn't see me at the beginning of the year, I could barely put my legs in the water." I let out a loud sigh. "I'm a really bad mermaid."

"No, you're not. It isn't your fault you never learned how to swim. Or that being turned was a traumatic experience. You're working with the tools that you were given."

"Well, they were rubbish."

He snorts. "Sorry."

"It's okay, it's kind of funny in a tragic way, can you imagine how ridiculous it's been for me to introduce yourself as a mermaid you can't swim?"

"*Couldn't*," he corrects. "You can now."

"True."

"And I guess I assumed you just didn't tell most people."

"I didn't. But sometimes you end up talking to people and it comes up naturally," I say, thinking back to my conversation with Bernie.

"I'm not going to even going to pretend to understand how that happened."

I shrug. "Have you never told anyone a secret of your own?"

"I guess I have." He takes a deep breath. "I hate dolphins."

I do a double-take, unsure if I heard him right. "What?"

"You were talking about secrets. Well, I hate dolphins."

"Okay, any particular reason?"

He glances down at his knees. "When I was six, I snuck off so I could go for a swim of my own while we were on holiday. I found a really cool reef and was exploring it."

"That sounds really fun."

He nods. "I think you'd like it. Well, anyway, after a while, this shadow gets cast over me. I panicked, thinking it was a shark, but when I looked up, it was a dolphin. It looked right at me, and seemed to smile."

"Can dolphins smile?"

"Honestly? I don't think so. But I was six, I had no idea what was really happening. It went on its way and did it's dolphiny thing while I went about my exploring. But then it came back. Every time it did, the shadow would fall over me and I'd start worrying about sharks, then the dolphin would smile at me again. Even if it wasn't really smiling, I'm certain it knew what it was doing. I could see it in its eye."

"That sounds horrible."

"It wasn't great," Wade admits. "After the fourth time, I decided it was time for me to leave and I made my way home. Mum was furious that I'd snuck off and I ended up grounded for the rest of the holiday. But she needn't have bothered, the dolphin freaked me out enough that it was years before I explored anywhere on my own again."

"I think I might dislike dolphins now too," I quip.

He lets out a warm laugh. "I appreciate the

solidarity. A lot of mer say that dolphins are great though, especially if you want to play with them."

"Maybe you came across a shifter and not a dolphin. You said it was on its own, that's weird, right? Dolphins normally move around in pods."

He raises an eyebrow.

"I watched a lot of nature documentaries about sea creatures after I was turned," I admit. "The water might scare me, but I still feel the call of the sea."

"Ah, understandable."

"I know."

"You might be right about it being a shifter, but I guess I'll never know unless I happen to come across a dolphin shifter bragging about how much he freaked out a mer thirteen years ago."

"That seems like an unlikely thing to happen," I admit.

"And yet it could."

I let out a small laugh. "I'll be sure to examine all future dolphin shifters I meet with suspicion until I find the one who wronged you."

"Ah, so this is why everyone says to get a girlfriend," Wade responds, amusement clear in his voice.

"Is that what I am?" My heart does a little flutter at the idea of it.

"I've never been the type to date around."

"Me neither. I don't see the point. Well, that's not true. I see the point for people who are poly. But I'm not, so I don't see the point for me. If I'm dating someone, then it's because I think it could be something." I tuck a strand of hair behind my ear and turn as far as I can in the bus seat so I can see him better. "So I guess, yes? I'm your girlfriend."

"And you'll fight dolphins for me?"

"I wouldn't go that far, I think they'd win."

"Mmm, they probably would. You can see it in their eyes."

I let out a light laugh. "How about I'll distract the dolphins so you can get away?"

"I could be okay with that."

I lean in and press my lips against his, feeling like I can deal with anything.

Even getting in the sea.

TWELVE

WADE

I STRIP off my clothing and put them in one of the lockers along the bank of the Humber. I sling my waterproof satchel over my shoulder and turn around to find a confused-looking Fiona watching everyone with her clothes bundled up in her arms.

"This locker's free," I say, gesturing to the one next to mine.

She nods. "I guess I'm just surprised that there's nothing here except a row of lockers." She shoves her clothes in and then pulls out her phone, adding that to the mix. "It's not a waterproof model."

"You should probably change that."

"I keep meaning to, but I never actually get around to it," she admits. "It hasn't been necessary."

"Ah, right. Is your bag waterproof?"

She nods. "I got it especially for the trip." She closes the locker and pulls out the key, slipping it into her bag and zipping it up. "I guess I expected there to be some kind of village here. Maybe for the mer who don't want to live underwater."

"Most of them just live among humans," I say. "But this place has been left just for mer to enter Merton." I reach out and take her hand in mine, leading her down the bank so she can get into the water.

One of the others takes a run up and jumps over us, transforming in the air and disappearing beneath with a flick of their fins.

Fiona's eyes widen and I can sense that she's starting to second-guess her decision to come on the trip.

"You don't have to do this if you don't want to," I say softly. "There's a village not far from here, we can walk and go get some cake or something."

"I want to see Merton," she says firmly, though I'm not sure if she's trying to convince herself, or me. I suppose it doesn't matter.

I nod and lead her closer to the water.

She fixates on it and tenses.

This is going to be harder than I expected it to be for her, she seems so at home in the pool.

Then again, she didn't drown in one. She drowned in the sea.

"Fiona, look at me?" I ask.

She meets my gaze and I can see all kinds of emotions swirling in her eyes, including fear and determination.

"This is your dolphin," I say.

Amusement quirks up the side of her lips.

"You said you'd help me with dolphins, well, I'm going to help you with this."

"I know."

"One step at a time." I squeeze her hand, wishing I could think of something to actually help her. "Try thinking of something good that happened in the water."

She raises an eyebrow. "I'm thinking about drowning."

"Is there anything you can think of instead? I know it's hard, but if you have a nice memory about the water, it might help."

She tears her gaze away from the water and meets mine. "I'm ready."

I hide my surprise, not expecting her to have one so quickly.

She lets go of my hand and steps into the water.

I hang back, partly to give her space, and partly because I want to be here in case she changes her mind and wants to turn around.

Fiona moves deeper into the water, running her hands across the surface. Her scales darken as she goes, and I can tell that she's still fighting the urge to let her tail out. Which is fair, I imagine being able to feel the bottom of the river is helping her right now.

She turns around to face me and gives me a shaky smile before dropping backwards into the water with a loud splash. The shimmering green scales of her tail flick up as she starts to move through the river.

Satisfied that she's doing okay, I hurry into the water, letting my tail free the moment that I can and swimming over to where she's keeping herself upright with her head above the water.

"I did it," she whispers.

I nod. "What did you think about?"

She bites her bottom lip and glances away.

"Sorry, I didn't mean to pry."

"It's not that. It's just that I thought about our first kiss. You said that I had to think about a good memory I had when it came to water, and that's what came to mind."

I move closer to her, reaching out and putting a

hand around her waist.

Fiona moves closer immediately and wraps her arms around my neck, clearly still thinking about our kiss.

"Want to make more good memories in the water?" I ask before realising how suggestive that sounds.

Her lips quirk up into a smile. "Maybe not when we have so many witnesses."

I raise an eyebrow. "I was talking about another kiss."

Amusement dances across her face. "I wasn't."

"Perhaps we should think about trying the normal way first."

"Maybe the normal way is in the water for mer." She's so close that I can feel her breath brush against my lips as she speaks. "It's a question I've never been able to find the answer to online."

I raise an eyebrow. "How much time have you spent looking for that?"

"Since my school friends started talking about it. There's surprisingly little about supernatural sex-ed on the curriculum."

I chuckle. "That's one way of putting it."

"I guess I just have a lot of questions about it. With humans these things are obvious, but I've seen you without any clothes on and..." she trails off. "Well, do you feel things the same way?"

Not for the first time, I find myself glad that mer don't have the same physiology as humans or she'd very much already know the answer to that question. "I suspect the answer is the same for you."

Her cheeks turn bright red. "I'm sorry, I guess I'm just curious."

"There's no need to be sorry," I assure her. "Asking is good. And if it helps, you're not the only one thinking about these things."

She raises an eyebrow. "You're thinking about the mechanics of mer sex?"

I chuckle. "No, I'm thinking about you."

She bites her bottom lip. "Then I suppose that's a good thing."

"It is. But if you're ready, we should head down to Merton. We only have a set amount of time before we have to get back on the bus."

"Right, Merton." From the expression on her face, it seems as if she's disappointed that we won't be spending more time just the two of us.

I can't say I feel differently, but I also don't want her to miss out on the thing she's been looking forward to.

"We'll have plenty of time later," I promise her.

"I'll hold you to that."

"You'd better." I lean forward and kiss her swiftly, not wanting her to lose too much concentration while we're out in open water. It's not the same as kissing when we're in the pool.

She pulls back and takes a deep breath, preparing herself for all of what's to come.

I do the same and dive under the water alongside her, excited for her to see my hometown for the first time.

THIRTEEN

FIONA

My natural instincts are making it fairly easy to make my way through the water, but even so, I keep finding myself looking over at Wade to check that I'm doing okay.

Every time I do, he smiles reassuringly at me, and I feel affection for him rise up within me. It would be easy for him to forget that I'm not as used to being in the water as he is, but he's keeping it in mind and going at a pace that's good for me.

He gestures to the left, and with a strong flick of my tail, I follow him down. The water is murkier than I expect it to be, but my eyes have easily adjusted to it, filtering out a lot of the dirt so I can see the silhouettes of the other MerSoc students who came with us.

Or maybe they're just other mer going about their business.

I follow Wade through a rocky circle and let out a small gasp as Merton comes into view. I'm not sure what I expected from the merfolk settlement, but what I can see in front of me is like everything I've ever imagined rolled into one.

Everywhere I look, there are people with all kinds of different tails, along with fish and other companions making their way about their day. Coral and sea plants line the walkways, and the buildings appear as if they're carved out of the seafloor itself. But it's far from primitive. There's a sense of grandeur to the whole place that is hard to ignore.

"Is it what you expected?" Wade asks.

I glance over at him, semi-surprised about how well I can hear him.

"Your ears are filtering out a lot of the water noise," he explains.

"How did you know that was what I was thinking about?"

"Partly your face, but I also guessed because you haven't spent much time underwater yet."

I nod. "I don't understand how we can speak and not drown."

"Because we've adapted to become better at surviving in our environment," he points out. "We're *supposed* to thrive down here, which means that we need to be able to talk without drowning ourselves."

"Right." It all makes so much sense but just isn't anything I've considered. At least I know that my complete lack of knowledge about the world I joined when I turned isn't a unique thing. Bernie seems to have gone through the same kind of thing when she became a vampire. I really wish I'd had someone who could have taken me through all of the changes that were happening to me, and answered the questions that came in droves.

Including those that I haven't had the need to know up until now. Until the past couple of weeks, I've not had much reason to worry about the mechanics of sleeping with someone beyond curiosity. I still don't have answers, but I suspect that won't be for too much longer.

"Are you feeling okay?" Wade asks, reaching out to touch my arm gently.

I nod. "I think so. I thought it would be harder than it is."

"It might hit you later," he says. "But hopefully once we're out of the water."

I nod, trying not to think about that too hard. Of all the things I expected to happen, I didn't take into account that I might have a delayed reaction to it all.

"Ready to go into the town?" he asks. "I'm guessing you've never tried kelp cakes?"

"I don't even know what they are."

"They're delicious, though I don't imagine they sound it to people who have grown up without them."

"I'm willing to try anything," I promise. "All of your delicacies."

He raises an eyebrow. "You might not like all of them."

"I'm sure I won't, but that doesn't mean I won't enjoy trying them. And for lunch, we can go to your favourite restaurant, if you want?"

"We can do that," he promises. "I'm guessing this is partly because you have no idea what to suggest we eat?"

"Partly. It's also because you light up when you talk about some things from Merton and I want to experience them myself."

"Then allow me to be your guide." He holds out his arm to me.

"Can we swim like that?"

"Easier than you might think."

I thread my arm through his and allow him to

guide me onto the main street of Merton. Everywhere I look, there are merfolk going about their daily lives with all kinds of tails. I wish I knew more about fish so I could recognise some of them, but I'm woefully ignorant about that.

A kiosk with a bubble above it catches my eye and I frown. "They're selling air?" I ask, gesturing to it.

Wade nods. "It's a temporary fix if you don't have time to go up to the surface. You can try it, if you want?"

"How long have we got until we need to surface for air?" I ask.

"Hmm, probably about forty-five minutes to an hour."

My eyes widen. "That short?"

He nods. "It's longer than dolphins."

"Ah, so your arch-rivals can be defeated, you just need to swim deeper."

"I had never thought of that," he admits. "See, you *have* protected me from dolphins."

"Only problem is that they're probably faster than we are."

"Mmm, you might be right about that. I've never tried to race one."

"Not even in the Obscure Academy pool?"

"I don't think there's ever been an inter-species race. At least not in our fully shifted forms."

"That feels like it's a fun competition the academy is waiting for," I respond.

"Careful, I think Georgie's influence is rubbing off on you. If you're not careful, you'll end up organising things," he teases.

"Then I'll just have to get her back for dragging me into helping her with the pool party by making her help me with my future event."

"Ah, a devious plan, I can get on board with that. Here we go, kelp cakes," he says, gesturing to a small bakery-style shop. "We should get some, then return to the surface to breathe, unless you want to try booth air."

"Do you recommend it?"

"Not really, but I know you want to try as much as possible."

"Then let's go to the surface this time. But maybe when we need to breathe again we can go."

He nods and leads me into the bakery.

A mermaid with shocking orange and white hair beams at us from behind the counter. "Good morning, what can I get you?"

"Can we have two kelp cakes to go, please?" he asks.

She nods and quickly removes them from the

sealed case, handing them to Wade in exchange for some coins.

"Thank you," he says, and leads me back out of the shop.

We go a little further down the street until we reach what looks like a stone bubble. He gestures for me to enter.

I frown, but do as he suggests, finding a small table and two benches waiting inside.

"It feels different in here," I say, holding out my hand. "But I can't explain why."

"It's magic," he responds. "These bubbles exist all over Merton, they're so you can do things like eat without getting the food drenched with saltwater. It's expensive to use the magic though, so most homes and businesses don't have it up. The bakery just has it in the counter where they keep the food."

"Oh, I hadn't thought of that."

"Not surprising, it's one of those things you don't consider until after you've been here." He hands me one of the cakes.

I unwrap it carefully, and lift it to my nose. It smells vaguely of salt, but other than that, I don't get much from it. With my curiosity well and truly piqued, I take a bite, surprised that the texture is rather pleasant on my tongue, almost like a brownie.

Wade bites into his own, eating it without the same reluctance as I have.

"What do you think?" he asks.

"It's good."

He beams. "These have always been my favourites. But we can try other things next time we're here so we can find yours."

"I'd like that," I respond, smiling at him.

I have to admit that despite being under the water, there's no doubt that I'm having fun. I'm sure there's going to be more work to make sure I'm completely over my fear of the open water, but this is a good step in the right direction. I've been making them ever since I arrived at Obscure Academy and decided that I was going to join MerSoc. The first time I encountered the pool I had the same sense of reluctance I felt before entering the estuary here.

Maybe in time, it'll disappear. So long as I keep facing my fear, that might actually be possible.

FOURTEEN

FIONA

WADE GESTURES TOWARDS THE SURFACE, making me more confused than ever about where we're going for lunch. I can't feel the burn in my lungs from not breathing yet, so I don't need air.

But maybe he needed to breathe. That would be a good reason for heading to the surface.

My head broke the water and despite not needing one, I took a deep breath. While it's less uncomfortable than I expected to spend so much time holding my breath, I can tell that I prefer being able to breathe normally.

"Ready to leave the water?" Wade asks.

"I thought we were going for lunch?"

"We are." He gestures to a stone building on a small island. "This is The Fin. It's only accessible to merfolk because of the approach, but it does some of the best grilled fish for miles around. I know you've only just started eating it again, so I thought you might want to come."

"It sounds interesting."

He pulls himself out of the water and onto one of the rocks, his tail disappearing as he does so. Wade reaches out his hand and I take it, focusing my energy on turning my tail back into legs so I can climb up after him.

"Is it okay that we don't have any clothes?" I ask, looking down at the scales still covering my body. I can make them disappear if I want to, but this seems to be my most natural state when I'm on land.

"There's only merfolk here," he reminds me.

"Right. I'm still not used to that, I feel very naked." It's only once I say the words that I realise I may have made the wrong decision in drawing attention to that.

"We can go somewhere else if you'd be more comfortable," Wade offers.

I consider it for a moment. I'm getting used to being like this around people, and the smell of grilled fish permeating the air is making my mouth water. "I'll be okay, I think."

"All right, but tell me the moment you change your mind." He entwines his hand in mine and draws me towards the restaurant.

Unsurprisingly, no one seems to even notice the fact I only have scales on, probably because everyone else does too. Though I hope for their own safety that the kitchen staff at least have aprons.

We're seated quickly and two menus appear. I scan down the items, not even having the slightest idea what to order.

"There are sharing platters if you want to try one of those," Wade says.

"There are?" I turn the menu over. "Ah, the seafood platter and the fish grill. Which would you prefer?"

"I don't mind. It's your first time here, not mine."

"And they're both good?"

He nods.

"Then I have the perfect way to choose." I lean down to my bag and pull out the Merton coin he gave me.

Wade gives me a curious look, but

understanding dawns on him when I hold it out. "You kept it?"

"Of course. Heads it's the seafood, tails it's the fish."

"Flip away."

I balance the coin on my thumb and attempt to flick it into the air, failing miserably in the process and the coin clatters to the table.

I let out an amused snort. "Well that went well."

"What does it say?"

"You're not going to listen to that terrible toss, are you?"

"The coin decided."

I let out a small laugh and lean over to see. "Tails. The fish it is."

Wade gets the attention of our waitress and orders swiftly.

"Thank you for bringing me here," I say. "I'm looking forward to trying the food." And I'm a lot more comfortable than I thought I'd be considering I don't have any clothes on.

"I think you'll like it. But if not, I have backup options to make sure you don't go hungry."

"It's been a nice day. Definitely a good break from lectures."

"You've never told me what you're studying," Wade says. "I guess I kind of assumed you were doing the same thing as I was, so didn't think to ask."

"Psychology," I answer.

His eyebrows shoot up.

"After I was turned, I needed help and I didn't get it. I know it sounds odd, but that kind of ignited my interest in psychology, so I took it as soon as I could at school. I want to train to be a therapist when I'm done with my degree. I don't know whether I want to specialise in exactly what I went through, but I do know that I want to work with children to help them work through their trauma. Maybe it's a strange response to drowning and turning into a mermaid, but that's where I'm at."

He reaches across the table and takes my hand in his, giving it a gentle squeeze. "I think it's a great thing to do."

I smile widely at him, pleased that he thinks so.

"Is there a service on campus for turned people?"

"I don't think so. It would be good if there was. You, Georgie, and the others have all done a good job helping me understand what it means to be mer, but I still wish I'd had somewhere else to ask some of the questions. And somewhere to talk to people who have had the same experience as I have."

He nods. "You should see if you can request one.

And if you can't, maybe you could set up an informal student group."

"I'm not sure TurnedSoc has a good ring to it."

"Hmm, you're right, it might need a different name. But if you want that to happen, then you could probably make it so that it does."

"I'll think about it. It would look good on any applications for further training I make," I muse.

"I was thinking more for helping you continue to get used to your life as mer, but that works too," Wade responds, amusement flitting through his voice.

"Stuff can be two things."

He chuckles. "Yes it can."

A huge platter of fish arrives before we can say anything else, and the waitress sets it down between us along with an array of sauces and sides.

My mouth waters, and I have to admit that it looks delicious.

"I've missed eating fish," I admit once she's gone. He already knows that, but I do want to reassure him that his choice of restaurant is a good one. "I feel like I have a whole new culinary world to discover by eating it."

"What's been your favourite so far?" he asks.

"I'll tell you once I've eaten this," I respond,

gesturing to the platter. "But when I was a kid, fish fingers."

"Have you ever had a fish finger sandwich?"

"I don't think so, though I'm not sure why."

"Then I'll make one for you when we're back at the academy."

"Sure. But just to be clear, we're talking about the breaded white fish sticks that go in the freezer, right?"

"We are."

"I'm not sure whether to be nervous or excited."

He chuckles. "If you go to a nice restaurant or café, they sometimes do a version with battered fish and fancy bread. I like them, but it's nothing compared to the cheap stuff smothered in ketchup. They're great for breakfast."

"You're not selling it," I tease, though maybe that's just because I haven't had them in years. "The food itself part. The idea of having breakfast with you is fun."

"Because you'll get answers to your questions?" His lips quirk up into a smile.

"I should warn you that I have many." I pick up a fork and eat a piece of the fish, enjoying how it melts in my mouth.

"Well, I hope I can help answer them, though I

fear you're going to be disappointed by how human it is."

A blush rises to my cheeks as I realise that I've backed myself into a corner where I have to admit to not having any experience with that way either. Though I suppose it's something I need to tell him anyway. I take a deep breath. "I've never slept with anyone," I blurt out. "So I have less than no expectations."

Slowly, Wade nods. "I don't know whether to say something suggestive or to be serious."

"You could try both?"

"That's one way of dealing with it, though I think I'll go with serious."

That's concerning. Is it a mistake to tell him about this?

He reaches over the table and puts his hand over mine. "If I ever do anything to make you uncomfortable..."

"You haven't," I assure him quickly.

"I'm glad. But if I do, then you have to tell me."

I nod. "It's not that I've never wanted to," I admit, feeling like it's a necessary part of the conversation. "I suppose I've just been very self-conscious about my scales and how someone would respond to them." Without meaning to, I touch the scales by my collarbone.

"I think your scales are beautiful."

I glance down at the platter. "I never thought about how you'd respond to them. I think it's all part of coming to terms with my mer side. It's not something I've had a lot of practice at, so I think I disliked that part of me. Or I suppose it's more like I've never had time to like it."

"But you do now?"

"I'm not sure," I admit. "I like parts of it. I feel beautiful when you look at me, and I'm enjoying being able to do things with all the other mer. So I think I'll get there. But there's still a part of me that's clinging on to how things could have been if I'd stayed human. I know that's not good, but sometimes I can't help it."

"You're only just learning to embrace your mer side," he says.

"Which is okay, right?"

"Of course it is. Everyone comes to terms with things like this in different ways and on different schedules. And for what it's worth, I'm glad that I get to be part of that for you."

"Me too." Even as I say the words, I'm certain they're true. And not because he taught me to swim either, it's so much more than that. And I hope he'll be able to help me answer more of my questions sooner rather than later.

Our conversation turns to the fish platter, and I find myself relaxing even more now that more of my situation is out in the open. I've never told anyone as much as I've told him, or Georgie, Melody, and Bernie. It seems that finding people who understand me has changed everything.

And I'm planning on embracing that with open arms.

FIFTEEN

WADE

THERE'S something surprisingly comforting about making drinks for two people in my own flat. Perhaps because it feels like such an everyday thing. This isn't about meeting for a date and each person trying to impress the other, this is about two people wanting to share a moment of their day with one another.

And about Fiona reading my new English essay for me. After all the help she's given me in order to help me understand exactly what's happening in the story, the least I owe her is a cup of tea and a fish finger sandwich. though I know she'll say that I don't owe her anything. I guess I did teach her how to swim, but that seems like a distant memory already, even if we still make use of the pool when it's just the two of us.

I enter my bedroom with two mugs and set one down in front of Fiona where she's sitting reading my essay. She smiles up at me and takes a sip, surprising me considering it's still so hot.

I sit down on my bed next to her, trying to contain my nerves over her response to what I've written. I know it's better than my first attempt, but whether it's good enough for my professor is another thing. Though I suppose she won't have any way of knowing whether that's the case or not.

"It's good," she says, setting her phone and her mug down on the desk. "I think you could be clearer on your point about Ophelia and the flowers, but I think your English professor will like it."

"That didn't take you long to get through." I drink the rest of my tea and put my mug down next to hers. Hmm, maybe it's been longer than I think it has.

"It was interesting to see your take on it," she responds.

"That's because it's mostly *your* take."

"Not true. It's your take on your understanding based on my take."

"Now that's just confusing. I'll see what I can do about the Ophelia part, but it might have to do."

"It's a shame there isn't a way for your professor to let you know if this is what he wanted."

"That would be too easy." I shuffle back on the bed and open my arm so she can come and sit with me.

"It would," she agrees, resting her head on my shoulder.

"Thank you for your help, I wouldn't have known where to start if you hadn't read my original essay."

"Which wasn't that bad, I don't know what your English professor is looking for, but he's an idiot for failing you based on that essay."

"You have to say that, you're my girlfriend."

"Nope, I don't. What's the point of building a relationship based on lies? Even if they're small ones."

"All right, that's fair." I trace my fingers up and down her shoulder absentmindedly. There's something comfortable about sitting here with her like this.

Or anywhere else. No one has ever made me feel the way that Fiona does. With her, the world goes quiet and all slips into place. I might not have any idea what I want to do with her life, and she might not have fully come to terms with what being mer means, but it feels right to be with her. Like we fit together, and everything else can just fall into place around it.

Not that it'll be easy to form a solid, healthy, relationship. If I want this to work long-term, then I need to put the effort in.

"What are you thinking about?" she asks.

"Hmm?"

"You seem lost in thought. What's on your mind? Is it your paper? We can go through the Ophelia scenes if you want, but I don't think it's necessary. You have a good grasp on it." She twists around so she's looking up at me, her shimmering green hair framing her face and her wide eyes making me feel like I'm the only person on her mind.

"I'm thinking about you."

"Oh." She tucks a strand of hair behind her ear. "What about me?"

"That I love you." The words slip out before I realise I'm saying them. And before I've given any thought to if she's ready to hear them. We've been dating for a couple of months already, but I have no idea if that's too soon.

I do know that I'm certain I mean them.

"I love you too," she responds. "It feels good to say it. I'm sure it's almost slipped out a couple of times already."

I raise an eyebrow. "It has?"

She glances down at the bedsheets and trails her fingers over the pattern there. "I definitely nearly said it last week when we were at the pool. It was the way you looked at me, and I just kind of knew," she admits.

I lean forward and capture her lips with mine, putting all of the emotions I'm feeling into the kiss. She shifts on the bed so she can wrap her arms around my neck and deepens the kiss.

Fiona breaks away from me, and starts to unbutton her shirt.

I reach out and gently catch her wrists. "We don't have to..."

"I know." Her hands fall away. "But I'm ready, Wade. I don't want to do this because I feel like I have to, or because someone else expects it. I want this. A lot."

I search her face, but it echoes what she's saying. "Then let me," I say, reaching out to touch her arm.

A smile spreads over her face, making her even more beautiful than before. I don't know whether it's because we've talked about this moment a lot, or if it's just because it's her, but it means even more to me than I thought it would.

This time, when I kiss her, neither of us stop. There's no need to when this is everything both of us want.

SIXTEEN

FIONA

IT ISN'T until I'm approaching the pool that I realise how excited I am to be going there. This is all Wade's doing. The water still scares me, but nowhere near as much as it did, and even if I'm feeling funny about the water, I do enjoy swimming, and not just because it means I get to spend time with Wade.

There's something about being in the water that isn't like anything I ever expected. The way I feel my tail move and my fins sway with the currents under the water is unlike anything I've ever felt, even when I showered before.

A loud splash comes from inside, and a smile pulls at my lips. Wade hasn't wasted any time jumping in and swimming.

I lean against the wall and watch him move through the water for a moment, admiring the way the muscles in his shoulders ripple, and the swish of his tail through the water as he moves. I don't think I'll ever get used to watching.

He turns around and spots me, coming to a standstill and waving at me.

"Hey," I say, quickly pulling my dress over my head.

His gaze bores into me, and even though I'm still covered in scales, I know what he's thinking.

And it's not fully appropriate for the pool. Or it wouldn't be if there were other people here.

I approach the edge of the pool.

"How was class?" Wade asks.

"It was good," I respond brightly.

"You're in a good mood," Wade says as I sit on the side.

"I am," I agree, leaning in and kissing him swiftly. "Why wouldn't I be when I get to spend the evening with you?"

He raises an eyebrow. "I didn't realise that a quick swim and then hanging out in my room was a good evening."

"That's a lie."

He chuckles. "That's fair. It's pretty great."

"Are you sure no one minds that we keep using the pool?" I ask. "It feels cheeky when all we're doing is just swimming."

"That's what the pool's here for," he points out. "We book the pool using the same system as all the other merfolk and water shifters. Anyone can do it."

"Do we have to pay for it?" I can't believe I've never thought about that possibility before, but if it's true, I need to fix it.

He shakes his head. "It's covered as part of our fees for being part of MerSoc."

"Huh, I never realised."

"Because you didn't read the fine print when you signed up?"

"Probably because I was super distracted by Georgie."

"Ah, yeah, I can imagine she was a little bit of a scatterbrain when she signed you up."

"She wasn't as smooth as she could have been, but I don't mind." Especially not when I got a good friend out of it.

"Mmm, me neither."

"I've been meaning to ask you though, what are you doing this summer? Do you have to work lots?"

"A bit, but nothing too bad. The thing about

teaching kids how to swim is that they all go on holiday in August."

"Oh, true, I hadn't thought of that," I say.

"Why?"

"My flatmates are hiring a beach house. Or one of them owns a beach house. I'm not even sure. There was something about a house and the seaside. I was wondering if you wanted to come."

"You don't mind me crashing?"

"I'm not the only one who'll be bringing someone. There'll be some group activities, some we can do on our own. A nice beach with some sea..."

"And you're actually looking forward to that?" he asks.

"Yeah, I am. Huh, I never thought I'd be saying that."

"A lot of things have changed since I came here," I admit. "Remember when you suggested I did something to help turned mer?"

"Vaguely, it's been a while."

"Bernie is a turned vampire," I say, knowing he'll remember her from the times they've met. "And we were talking about things and then things kind of escalated to the point where we were saying that we wished there'd been something for us when we'd been turned." I slip into the water between his arms, enjoying the position it puts me in.

"So you set one up, right?" he guesses.

I smile, pleased at how well he knows me. "We're almost there," I respond. "We had a meeting with the Student Union rep and have filled out all the paperwork. Whether it'll be anyone other than the two of us is another matter. But if it is, we'll be able to help people, both with the emotional part, and the practical part."

"You mean like explaining the mechanics of certain things?" he jokes.

"I know you're trying to make a joke, but yes, including that. Though I'll admit there are still things I'm curious about."

"I'd have thought my teachings were even more thorough than for swimming."

"I have to say I'm equally pleased with both," I tease.

He chuckles and leans closer. "Then I'm going to have to try harder."

"I'm not going to complain about that." I press my lips against his, kissing him deeply. It's hard to believe how well we've managed to fit together.

He pulls back and cups my cheek in his hands. "I'm really glad you told me about your swimming problem."

"Me too." I meet his gaze, losing myself in the way he's looking at me.

I've never doubted my academic path, but before I came to Obscure Academy, I had no idea what was happening in my personal life. I didn't know how to be a mermaid. I couldn't swim, I had no idea about all kinds of things that I should have done because of who I was. And I'm not the only one, it seems. I don't even have to wait for the end of my education to start helping people in the same position as I am. Or people who are in Bernie's.

It's funny how things turn out. I know that I've got my whole life ahead of me, but it feels like I'm off to a pretty good start.

EPILOGUE

FIONA

Several Months Later

A LOUD SPLASH fills the air as one of the mer jumps into the pool, sending droplets of water into the air. One of them lands on my face, and I close my eyes, enjoying the feel of it.

I never thought I'd feel this way while around water, but there's no denying that there's something comforting about being around it.

I swish my tail through the water and lean back as I wait for Wade to come back from the drinks table.

"I brought you a drink, I saw you didn't have one," Wade says as if summoned by my thoughts.

I open my eyes and smile widely at him. "Thank you." I take it from him and pop it open.

"Can I sit here?"

I chuckle at the memory of the first time we met. There's something endearing about him recreating it, even if he does the same every few weeks. I wave to the spot at the side of the pool and he sits down, letting his tail spring forth the moment it hits the water.

"Cheers," he says, holding out his can to me.

I knock my own against it. "Cheers."

He puts his arm around me and I lean against him, resting my head on his chest and enjoying the atmosphere.

Georgie waves at me from across the pool and dives in, making her way over with a few quick flicks of her tail.

"Hey guys," she says as she hoists herself out of the pool and sits. "Are you ready for the holidays?"

I nod. "I'm going to miss this, though," I admit, surprising even myself with that.

"Oh, I know. But we'll be back next year," she assures me. "Do you have any plans for the summer yet?"

I glance at Wade and nod. "I'm going to Merton

for a week to meet Wade's family properly. And my flatmates are all going to Whitby for a week."

"Oh, when?"

I frown and look at Wade.

"Third week of July," he responds.

"Thanks, I've never been very good with keeping dates straight," I respond.

"That's so funny, a few of us are going then too," Georgie responds. "We should meet up and have an Obscure Academy house party or something."

"That sounds like fun. We were already planning on doing something like that. I'll message you about it when I find out the actual details."

"I'll hold you to that," she responds brightly. "Hey, Ben, Felix, stop it!"

Her shout to the mermen draws my attention to where they seem to be getting a little too handsy with each other.

Georgie groans. "I swear it was better when they were fighting all the time," she mutters.

"You must have a nightmare of a time in the sea," Wade jokes.

She throws him an unimpressed look. "I try not to think about it very much," she admits.

"That's probably for the best," he agrees. He raises an amused eyebrow at me, and it's all I can do to smother a giggle.

"But right now, I'm going to go break them up so that we don't have to." She jumps back into the water and heads in their direction.

"I never asked how the two of you know each other," I say to Wade.

"We grew up together."

"Oh. And you never thought about..." I trail off, not knowing whether I should be asking the question I have on my mind.

"Of dating each other? Not really. We did get fake married when we were five though."

A slight jolt of jealousy shoots through me but I push it to the side. "I'm not going to find out that means something to merfolk, am I?"

Wade lets out an amused chuckle. "About as much as it means to humans when they do it. But there's never been anything between me and Georgie. She's just a friend. And I'm not saying that in a weird I-wish-she-was-more way. There's only one mermaid I'm interested in."

"Oh?"

"Mmhmm. She had a slow start when it came to using her fins, but she's brave and beautiful."

"Is that right?" I ask, a wide smile spreading over my face.

"It is." His eyes soften as he looks at me, and I can sense him starting to lean in.

My eyes flutter closed as his lips meet mine and I wrap my arms around his neck, pulling him closer. He deepens the kiss, not caring who can see.

If we're not careful, Georgie will be coming over to tell us off as well.

We break apart, and I don't need to see my face to know I'm smiling broadly. I can see the same expression on Wade's face.

"I love you," he says.

"I love you too," I respond.

"Wade, Fiona, are you joining for water polo? We need two more?" Georgie calls from across the pool.

Wade looks at me. "What do you say?"

"That I'm still not sure of the rules, but I'm not going to let that stop me," I respond brightly.

He chuckles. "We're going to lose so badly."

"But the point is to have fun in the water, right?" I dip my hand into the water and splash it up at him.

He returns the favour and I let out a loud laugh, feeling more carefree than I have in years.

I had high hopes when I came to Obscure Academy, but even I have to admit that my first year here has far outweighed them, and I can't wait to find out what I'll do next.

* * *

Thank you for reading *Flipping Tails For Seasick Mermaids*, I hope you enjoyed it! If you want to continue the series, you can with *Potion Making For Disastrous Witches*, which follows Michaela as she searches for help with one of her potions: http://books2read.com/potionmakingfordisastrouswitches

If you want to find out how Fiona and Georgie met and how Fiona signed up for MerSoc, you can find out by downloading a free bonus prologue: https://books.authorlauragreenwood.co.uk/e370jffewp

Thank you for reading *Flipping Tails For Seasick Mermaids*, I hope you enjoyed it!

In my original plan for the *Obscure Academy* series, Fiona didn't actually have a book of her own (though she did have a side story), but the series kind of took on a life of its own once I started writing it, and I realised that it wouldn't be right to not give Fiona a book of her own. It was also a little down to my partner wanting to see the drunk-mermaid-in-the-shower scene that I reference in *Potion Making For Disastrous Witches* (which is actually the second book I wrote for the series, even though it's the fourth book overall).

The merfolk that Wade mentions in chapter 4 are all real legends of half-people, half-fish, from around the world. Sirens are from several different mythologies, merrows and ceasgs are from Celtic lore, rusalkas from Slavic lore, renyu is one of the names for Chinese mermaids, and ningyo is a type of Japanese mermaid. There's already a siren in my world (Melody in *Enchanting Songs For Silent Sirens*), and I do intend on exploring more of the lore surrounding other types of merfolk in the future.

If you want to keep up to date with new releases and other news, you can join my Facebook Reader Group or mailing list.

Stay safe & happy reading!

- Laura

Signed Paperback & Merchandise:

You can find signed paperbacks, hardcovers, and merchandise based on my series (including stickers, magnets, face masks, and more!) via my website: https://www.authorlauragreenwood.co.uk/p/shop.html

Series List:

* denotes a completed series

The Obscure World

A paranormal & urban fantasy world where supernaturals live out in the open alongside humans. Each series can be read on its own, but there are cameos from past characters and mentions of previous events.

Cauldron Coffee Shop - Broomstick Bakery - Obscure Academy - The Shifter Season - Grimalkin Academy* - City Of Blood* - Grimalkin Vampires* - Supernatural Retrieval Agency* - Sabre Woods Academy* - Scythe Grove Academy*

* * *

The Forgotten Gods World

A fantasy romance world based on Egyptian mythology.
Each series can be read on its own, but there are cameos
from past characters and mentions of previous events.

Forgotten Gods

The Egyptian Empire

A modern fantasy world set in an alternative timeline
where the Egyptian Empire never fell.

The Apprentice Of Anubis

The Paranormal Council Universe

A paranormal romance & urban fantasy world where
paranormals are hidden away from the human world,

and are in search of their fated mates. Each series can be read on its own, but there are cameos from past characters and mentions of previous events.

The Paranormal Council Series* - Paranormal Criminal Investigations* - The Necromancer Council*

Other Series

Amethyst's Wand Shop Mysteries (with Arizona Tape) - Purple Oasis (with Arizona Tape) - Grimm Academy - Beyond The Curse* - The Vampire Detective* (with Arizona Tape) - The Dragon Duels* - Speed Dating With The Denizens Of The Underworld (shared world) - Seven Wardens* (with Skye MacKinnon) - Firehouse Witches* (with Lacey Carter Andersen & L.A. Boruff)

ABOUT LAURA GREENWOOD

Laura is a USA Today Bestselling Author of paranormal, fantasy, urban fantasy, and contemporary romance. When she's not writing, she drinks a lot of tea, tries to resist French macarons, and works towards a diploma in Egyptology. She lives in the UK, where most of her books are set. Laura specialises in quick reads, whether you're looking for a swoonworthy romance for the bath, or an action-packed adventure for your latest journey, you'll find the perfect match amongst her books!

Follow the Author

- Website: www.authorlauragreenwood.co.uk
- Mailing List: www.authorlauragreenwood.co.uk/p/mailing-list-sign-up.html
- Facebook Group: http://facebook.com/groups/theparanormalcouncil

- Facebook Page: http://
  facebook.com/authorlauragreenwood
- Bookbub: www.bookbub.com/authors/
  laura-greenwood